CW00666083

Stories from the
Microbial World

---

edited by D. A. Baden

Habitat Press

Habitat Press

Foreword

With the support of the University of Southampton, I founded the Green Stories project to encourage writers to embed 'green' solutions into stories aimed at mainstream readers, or to create visions of what a sustainable society might look like if we did things right. Since it was founded in 2018, a variety of sponsors have enabled us to run twenty free competitions which have given rise to several publications, plays and scripts.

One of these sponsors was the Environmental Biotechnology Network (EBNet) which is funded by UKRI. In 2023 EBNet sponsored a short story competition on the theme of 'Microbes to the Rescue!' When many people think of 'microbes' they think of germs, bacteria, nasty tiny little things that cause trouble. But they can be our friends. They are like mini magicians, breaking down food waste into rich compost, transforming human and animal waste, even pesticides and pollution into harmless, often even useful substances.

From the original 161 entries, we have picked fourteen to showcase the wide variety of perspectives on our microbial world. Some stories, such as 'What Any Fool Can Do' are written by experts in the field and give an accurate and fascinating insight into the microbial world. But they are all works of fiction, and mostly the science takes second place to the plot. We've selected stories from a variety of genres, mostly aimed at adults.

We begin, however, with six stories from our 'Clean vs Green' short story competition which similarly uses fiction to tackle myths and misconceptions about bacteria. The goal was to raise awareness of the environmental and health implications of over-cleaning. Many of us are now aware of the 'beneficial bacteria' in our gut, yet still scrub off all the friendly bacteria on our skin that has evolved to keep our skin healthy and clean. Persuaded by misleading marketing blurb claiming 'this kills 99% of all germs', we expose our lungs and environments to sometime dangerous levels of volatile organic compounds. Indeed, most information reaching the public about cleaning has come from the advertising industry, not health professionals. We hope that these stories help to redress the balance as well as entertain.

We finish with two stories adapted from the novel 'Habitat Man' which show in amusing ways how micro-organisms help us process waste. 'The Pitch' begins with a plea for costing for nature accounting approaches and finishes with a pitch for a composting toilet - possibly the ultimate metaphor for the circular economy! 'The Polyamorist' takes a fun look at home-composting... amongst other things.

As authors came from across the world, with different spelling and grammar conventions, we have chosen to keep their original formats.

Contents

The Society for Organ Welfare

by Adrian Ellis

The sun was shining as I walked towards the building that housed the Society for Organ Welfare. It was a two-storey, brick-and-wood building, sitting amongst thick woodland. I walked across its drive and stepped through its front door into a cool, shady foyer. I greeted the receptionist, gave her my name, and was directed to Dr Kindred's office on the first floor.

Dr Kindred was sitting on a wooden chair by a round table when I entered. She was middle-aged, healthy-looking, and she had an air of calm authority. Through her rear window, trees swayed in the morning breeze. Her office contained hessian rugs, bare floorboards, unpainted wooden furniture and pot plants. She greeted me and motioned for me to sit on the opposite chair. I took my seat, feeling uncomfortable. She picked up her tablet device and studied its screen.

I waited, drumming my fingers, then I blurted out, 'is my liver coming back to me?'

'No,' she replied, 'not at the moment, Mr Lorber. Your liver doesn't feel sufficiently safe to return to you. It is still recovering from your abusive treatment. It wishes time alone.'

'But that's crazy! I can't carry on doing this special diet you've put me on...' I waved my hands at my abdomen. 'With a synthetic organ inside me forever! I've stopped drinking. What more does it *want*?'

'When we scanned your body, two years ago, Mr Lorber, with our organ communication system, your liver cried out to us. It had been abused for years and was in a physically poor state. It had been overworked, denied basic nutrition, and was severely injured. Your defence,' she glanced at her tablet, 'that your liver had "made no complaint" is, sadly, the mentality of any abuser who damages and inflicts suffering on those who cannot fight back or even vocalise their pain.'

I rolled my eyes. 'I didn't even *know* it was suffering. I was just having a good time, doctor. I was partying, socialising. I had a few hangovers, but that was it!'

'We know that,' she replied. 'Your brain told us the details. It also reported that you inflicted many dangerous and traumatic impacts on it during your sports activities. Fortunately for you, it wishes to stay with you.'

'Well, bully for my brain! *It* can't leave me!'

She looked coolly at me. 'At the moment, no. But that may change. There is evidence that certain individuals can function by only using a primitive brain stem.' She glanced at me. 'It seems possible.'

I frowned. 'So nothing's changed?' Hey... wait. If that's the case, why did you call me here this morning?'

'Because another of your organs is crying out in distress.'

'Which one? My lungs?'

'No.'

'Spleen?'

'No.'

'Gall bladder?'

'No.'

I grimaced. 'I'm running out of organs.'

'It's your skin.'

I stared at her. 'But that's not an *organ,* that's just a... covering.'

She closed her eyes for a second, then looked at me. 'Mr Lorber, your skin is much more than a covering. It is your largest organ. It carries out crucial activities to keep you healthy and survive. It handles temperature regulation, water regulation and protects your body from pathogens.'

'You mean viruses and bacteria?'

'Yes, along with fungi and mites.'

'Right, you mean the evil things.'

She narrowed her eyes. 'Mr Lorber, bacteria aren't evil. Neither are fungi. They are like people. Some are dangerous, just as some people are dangerous, but most of them are not. The idea that all bacteria are nasty is like saying the entire human race should be destroyed because some of them are serial killers. Mr Lorber, your skin contains a forest of bacteria.'

'Yuck!'

'But that is the *only* way your body stays healthy,' she added. 'It needs many types of bacteria. Different bacteria colonise different areas. Some are very specialised. For example, certain bacteria *only* live in your belly-button, whereas others are found throughout your body. They defend you. They attack foreign invaders that try to break through your skin and make you ill. They are your castle guards and you have been attacking them. By using excessive amounts of disinfectants and anti-bacterial soaps on your skin, you've severely damaged your skin's natural defences. In your foolish efforts to stop invaders, you've ended up massacring your own castle guards.'

'Oh,' I said.

'Do you have cracked-skin problems?'

'Yes.'

'Eczema?'

'Yes,' I replied, 'but I thought that was because I *hadn't* used enough antibacterial...'

'Your skin was weeping, *literally*, when we scanned it, Mr Lorber. It is not a healthy forest anymore, it's more like a rubbish-strewn car park. You need to help it become a forest again. You need to expose it to a healthy, natural environment. Do some gardening, grow plants, play in the woods. Cut down on your disinfectant use. If you're worried about bacterial and viral infections, buy healthier meat, or less meat, or possibly no meat at all. A study by environmental scientists discovered that poor standards at slaughterhouses meant that there were more dangerous, animal faecal bacteria in people's kitchen sinks than in their toilet.'

'Yuck!'

'Yes.'

'So...' I looked at my hands. 'Is my skin going to leave me?' I went cold. 'Oh my God, if that happened, I'd be flayed alive!'

'We won't be taking your skin away, Mr Lorber, but we will be monitoring the situation. If your behaviour doesn't improve, you'll have to spend time in one of our biome centres.'

I grimaced. 'Those hippy prisons?'

'Healthy biome centres are *not* hippy prisons. Many people who spend time there can't believe how much healthier and happier they've become. Let your skin's forest do its job. The woods are dirty, but that doesn't mean they're sick. They contain vibrant, healthy creatures. Trust in your body's ability to protect itself.'

'Right,' I said.

She tapped on her tablet. 'Returning to the matter of your liver, I'm booking a session in which you and it can spend some time together, under supervision. There'll then be a period of digestion and reflection on both parts. If that progresses well, we can move to the next step.'

'Right.'

'Okay,' she said. She put down her tablet device. 'That's everything for today, Mr Lorber. You'll need to come back next week for a skin test. Hopefully, by then, it'll be happier.'

'Yes. Thank you, Dr Kindred.' I stood up and left the room.

I walked down the stairs, crossed the foyer, and left the building. I headed back to town, the sun bright over my head. I looked down at my bare arms as I walked. I thought for a second, then I crossed the road and continued my journey on the shady side of the street.

The New Normal

by Rab Ferguson

I t was the avocado that changed everything. Before that, Willow was able to pretend things were fine. It was just her and Dad, looking after each other, the same as always. If it hadn't been for the avocado, maybe nothing would have changed – and she might never have seen a glass of orange squash bigger than she was!

How they did the groceries used to feel normal. Willow and Dad went round the shop together, getting everything on Dad's list, while she also chipped in with "helpful" suggestions like buying more chocolate cereal. Then when they arrived home, they'd put it all away. The tins went in the tin cupboard, the fruit in the fruit bowl, and the milk in the fridge. Simple.

A lot had happened since then. There'd been social distancing, and school being closed, and school being back but in "bubbles". Now, everything had settled into the *new normal* instead. For example, when they got back in the car after the shop:

"We almost lost the patient," Dad said, lowering his face mask and pretending to be a surgeon.

"Luckily, I got the stitches done just in time,' Willow played along.

That sort of thing felt *almost* like the old normal to Willow. Her and Dad messing around as usual. It was once they got the shopping inside that things got really weird.

"Time for the wipes!" Dad said, getting out packets of anti-bac wipes. He said it like it was a joke, but they did actually wipe everything down. The tins of beans, the apples for the fruit bowl, even the plastic milk bottles. The wipes made everything damp and shiny and smell like chemicals.

Dad wiggled his eyebrows at Willow, as if to say, *can you believe we're doing this?* Some of her friends had told her they'd done this sort of thing too, at the start of the pandemic. But they said it like it was some crazy story from the past – while Willow and Dad were still sterilising the shopping, and had been for two years now. It wasn't just the groceries either. Twice a day, Dad cleaned the floor and sides with a strong-smelling bleach that made her head spin. He'd also started washing their clothes at a higher temperature, and with more detergent, which was making them itchy and too small.

It was hard for Willow to know if his cleaning was too much. Even adults couldn't agree what the right things were to do around Covid, so how was she supposed to know? But that day, when she watched Dad rub an anti-bac wipe over an avocado, something just felt wrong. She was sure that couldn't be necessary – in fact, she was worried that putting those chemicals on fruit could be bad for them. Really, it was the avocado that set everything in motion – including the bizarre events of later that evening!

Willow knew why Dad worried about germs and getting ill. If he was ill, who'd look after Willow, and make sure they had everything they needed? Dad might make a lot of jokes, but he'd looked after her by himself since she was little. It was the one thing he *was* serious about.

Of course, she was old enough to pretty much look after herself now. But that wasn't something Dad saw. In his eyes, she was still the same little girl she'd been in primary school – or even nursery! But she was more grown up now, and it was her job to look after him too.

That evening, when Dad thought she was doing her homework, Willow went on her tablet and looked up the cleaning products they had in the house: the ones that boasted about how they killed 99.9 percent of germs. As she read, she drank from a glass of orange squash. She had no idea of the amazing journey this little bit of research was going to send her on!

Willow ended up reading for ages, the sky getting darker outside. What she learned was fascinating. It turned out there were good bacteria on her body, which helped protect against germs that could make her sick. The anti-bac bleaches and wipes got rid of the good bacteria too.

Her eyelids were getting heavy, but she was determined to keep reading. Normally, Dad would have already come up to check that she was asleep, but he was absorbed in a history documentary. He was a funny one, Dad. He couldn't pay attention for a full superhero movie, but he could easily watch a two-hour documentary about the history of paint.

Willow read about probiotic cleaning products next. They were cleaning sprays, laundry detergents and wipes that didn't use chemicals to kill the germs in the same way, and actually supported the good bacteria. There were all sorts of tips online around how to keep the good bacteria alive, like putting the clothes wash on a lower heat, or washing your hands with soap rather than using anti-bac hand gel. Willow was thinking about those "good germs" when she felt her head drop forward and her eyes close, as if of their own accord.

She opened her eyes again, and everything looked different. It took her a moment to figure out how. Everything was bigger. Her tablet was as wide as a dinner tray. Her chair was taller, so her feet no longer touched the floor. Her orange squash glass was bigger than her head. Even the walls and floor had grown, like her room was expanding away from her.

Wait, no. Everything else wasn't bigger. She was smaller! Willow felt another shrinking sensation. Now, the tablet looked more like a surfboard, and the squash glass was towering over her. The drop from her chair to the floor had become frighteningly long. It happened again, and she couldn't even see the tablet anymore – just the underside of her gigantic desk. The edges of the chair were so far away they looked like horizons. She was the size of an insect now!

With a final lurch, she became so small she could no longer see the edges of the chair. Instead, there was flat land stretching out all around her. Crawling across the land, there were bizarre creatures of all shapes, sizes and colours. Some were incredibly hairy, and were actually pulling themselves along with their own hairs! Others looked like one BIG hair, snaking and twisting around. Some were translucent, and jelly-ish, and looked as if they'd be sticky to touch.

It was like being on an alien farm, but Willow knew she wasn't looking at extraterrestrials. She was so small she could see bacteria! Then one in particular caught her eye. It was a huge pile of purple-ish slime, which contracted and pulsed as it moved – and it was heading directly towards her!

Panicking, Willow turned and headed the other direction, stumbling through a bunch of cat-sized worm creatures, then dodging round a large bacteria that looked like an undersea plant. She glanced over her shoulder, and the morphing mound of slime was chasing right behind her!

Looking back caused Willow to trip, falling over one of the worm creatures before landing in a heap on the ground. The slime slurped towards her, showing no signs of slowing down as she struggled to get back to her feet. It was going to absorb her right into its sticky mess!

A stream of emerald water washed and crashed in front of her, causing the jiggling slime to stop. The emerald water rose up like a backwards waterfall, forming into an almost humanoid shape. Something about this dripping guardian made the slime sink back, then slug away in a different direction.

"Thank you," she said to the watery humanoid, though she said it a little hesitantly. She didn't know if it was able to hear her, or if it had only saved her for itself anyway.

It would not hurt you, Willow, said its voice – inside her head! *Only very few bacteria are dangerous.*

Willow looked over skeptically at the slime dragging itself away from them. "Well, still, thank you anyway. I'd prefer not get covered in whatever that's made of."

We will always protect you. In a way, we are part of you. But we've brought you here because we need your help, the bacteria said.

"Who's we?" Willow replied. It felt almost like a snarky answer, but this wasn't a situation she'd been in before!

I believe you call us... the good bacteria.

"I was just reading about you," said Willow. In an odd way, it felt like meeting a celebrity. "Well, it sounds like you do a lot for me, and keep me healthy. What can I do for you?"

Our world has become too dangerous. This is why we called you here.

Willow looked around and realised it wasn't only her emerald water guardian she was speaking to. Bacteria had circled around her, in all different colours, shapes and sizes. This voice she was hearing was all of them speaking together. It blew her mind to think that these were her own bacteria, who lived on her body and kept her healthy.

Please. Look after us as we look after you. The chemicals are destroying too many of us. If this goes on, we will not be able to protect your health.

"It's Dad. He's been worried about getting ill. But he doesn't realise that he's actually making it more likely!"

You must save us.

"But how?" asked Willow. How could she stop Dad when he was trying his best to look after them both?

You must, the bacteria repeated. A watery emerald strand extended out from her guardian, reaching out and connecting with her hand. It felt cold and damp as it made contact with her skin. Willow began to grow bigger, all the bacteria vanishing, her desk and tablet coming back into sight, her chair becoming the correct size under her. Then she lifted her head, and it felt like waking up.

But had she really just woken up? It had seemed so real. And her hand still felt cool where the emerald bacteria had touched it. There was one thing she knew for certain. She needed to talk to Dad.

Willow stood outside the front room door in the dark with her tablet in her hand. She could see the light of the TV under the door, and hear Dad's history documentary. The presenter was talking at length about how grain was grown in medieval England.

"How can he watch two hours of this?" Willow muttered to herself. In reality, though, she was feeling nervous. Which was weird, because it was only Dad! But apart from making jokes about it, he'd never really talked about the extra cleaning he was doing. It was like she was bringing up something personal, and possibly upsetting.

Willow took a deep breath and stepped into the front room. Dad was in his chair, and he muted the TV, where the history presenter was standing in front of a field of wheat.

"Sneaking down to listen to my history documentary?" Dad asked, raising his eyebrows.

"No. Surprisingly not." Willow replied. But then she didn't know how to phrase what she was going to say next. "I just wanted to tell you... er... a lot of bacteria are actually good."

Dad stared at her for a long moment, looking as confused as he would if she'd come downstairs and started speaking in French. Willow's stomach twisted. This already felt like it was going badly.

"Um... what?" Dad asked eventually.

"We use cleaning stuff that get rid of 99.9% of bacteria. But we're getting rid of the good bacteria that keep us healthy," said Willow. Then she told him what she'd learned about bacteria, and the different types of cleaning products, and how to keep their surfaces and clothes clean in a healthy way. She didn't mention her maybe-a-dream. She didn't think that would help her case.

"It's great that you're taking an interest in science." Something in the way Dad said it made Willow's heart sink. "But we need to use those cleaners. It's about keeping us safe, with the way the world is now. "

Willow was gutted. She'd told him everything, and he'd shut her down straight away. It was like his mind was already made up, and it didn't matter what she said.

"Covid doesn't change the fact we need good bacteria," she said, determined to get through to him. "In fact, it makes it even more important!"

"Look," Dad sounded defensive, and like he was getting annoyed. "This isn't something you need to be worrying about."

"But I do worry about it. We've only got each other. And it could make one of us sick."

"Don't be silly, Willow. We're not going to get sick because things are clean."

She felt her face burn hot with frustration. "I'm not the one being silly."

"I make the decisions in this house." Dad was properly angry now. "It's an adult problem, and I'll deal with it as I see fit."

"It's not an adult problem, it's a you problem!" Willow burst out.

Dad looked shocked. For a moment, she thought he was going to shout back at her. But Dad wasn't like that.

"We're not talking about this anymore." His firm tone left no space for argument. "Go to your room. And I don't want to hear about it tomorrow either."

Dad turned off the television and put the remote down on the sofa. He left the front room, leaving Willow standing alone with tears in her eyes, feeling utterly stuck. He wasn't willing to change his mind.

"I don't know how to help," she whispered to herself, wondering if somewhere the good bacteria were listening.

But the next morning, something was different. When Willow woke up, she could smell lemons. Not a chemical lemon cleaner scent – actual fresh lemons.

She found Dad downstairs in the kitchen. He was doing the cleaning, but not with the usual bleach and wipes. He had bicarbonate of soda and lemons on the side, and was pouring white vinegar into a spray bottle.

"I read about this online," Dad said, smiling and showing the spray bottle to Willow. "It's a way of cleaning that doesn't damage those good bacteria. I've put on a wash too, on a lower heat, with a bit less detergent. And I've ordered some of those probiotic cleaners you told me about."

"Thanks Dad," she said. He'd actually listened to her!

"You're welcome. And, uh, I'm sorry about last night. I shouldn't have responded like that."

"That's okay," Willow said.

Dad sat down at the table, that was now damp and shiny, and smelled of real lemons. He gestured for Willow to sit opposite him.

"I know my cleaning's got a bit much," he said, once she'd sat down. "I'm going to talk to somebody about it, and see if I can get some help. In the meantime, I thought I'd try to use more of these healthier ways of cleaning. Maybe we can learn more about them together?"

"That sounds brilliant, Dad."

The new normal was very strange. But as she and Dad chatted about how they'd start cleaning in a safer way, Willow began to think that maybe "new" wasn't so bad after all. Especially when her Dad and the good bacteria were all looking after each other!

Mostly For You

by Jenni Clarke

Miriam stared into her morning coffee. Last night's date was the best and the worst she'd ever experienced. She was never dating again.

Jerry was a feast for the eyes and mind. She couldn't remember how many topics they'd discussed, only that he'd listened to her opinions as if they mattered rather than bulldozing through her words. It felt like she'd known him forever.

She swiped a tear from her cheek in annoyance. One evening with a man was not worth heartache, and yet she was crying into her coffee, stomach too knotted to eat, brain rehashing everything.

Miriam's flatmate thumped her shoulder

'Girl, why are you still here? You'll be late for work.'

Miriam glanced at the clock on the wall and swore. Her first client was a dragon, but she paid well. She couldn't lose this job mooning over a man she'd just met.

'You best cough up later, girl.'

Miriam grabbed her keys. 'Sure, I will. Pizza and beer? My treat.' She hurried down the stairs.

Her little car coughed into life and Miriam thanked the car gods. She wished she could afford a new one. Her blue beast drank fuel and spat out more nasties than she was happy with, but the rising living costs meant her meagre savings were melting away like an ice cube on a hot bonnet.

'Oh, come on,' she shouted at the slow driver in front. 'You could get a bus through there.' She slapped her hands on the wheel, tension building through her body. One minute late, and she'd lose money. One minute.

A gap in the traffic allowed her to risk overtaking, although it meant giving the other driver heart palpitations. A horn blared behind her, but she zipped away, almost running a red light before swerving into the avenue and slamming her brakes on to avoid hitting Buster. Killing her client's pet would not be a good idea, even if it meant less cleaner for her.

Miriam parked in the driveway with seconds to spare, but still had to grab her cleaning equipment and hurry to the back of the house and through the utility door, ready to blast away any dirt or germs. She never skimped on the products she used, but after last night, she shuddered at the amount of harsh chemicals in her box.

Her client's scowl and tapping foot told her all her efforts had been in vain. It didn't matter how strong or expensive her cleaning products were, it would not be good enough. She was late. There would be a speck of dust somewhere, a smear on a mirror, or an imagined crumb wedged in a corner. A reduction would be demanded, and one rule of being a self-employed cleaner was you never argued with your client.

Miriam dumped pizza and two opened beers onto the table in front of Rose and flopped onto the sofa.

'Spill, girl,' Rose said, grabbing a slice and waving it in Miriam's face. 'And don't skimp on the details or fob me with nothings. I saw your glum this morning.'

Miriam laughed. 'Great date, hottie, conversation, no awkwardness, perfect, disaster.'

Rose picked up both beers and held them out of Miriam's reach.

'Okay. He was lovely, we chatted about everything, and he listened. Can you imagine? He didn't steer the conversation back to himself or football. He listened. And his big brown eyes that saw me and didn't judge, well I guess they did in the end, and he has gorgeous hair, natural, you know and sort of flopping in his eyes.' She stopped as Rose passed her a bottle and laughed.

'You dated a puppy, girl?'

'Ha, no. Maybe I should next time.' She grabbed a slice of pizza.

'Why no rematch?'

Miriam shook her head. 'You should've seen the disgust on his face when I told him I was a cleaner.'

'Get out. What a snob. You're better off without that one, babes.'

'No, not a snob. He cares about the environment.' Miriam explained what had happened, and her stomach ached at the thought of never seeing him again. 'He's got a point, too. I looked it up when I got home.'

'What you on, sister? The man trashed your hard-earned business.'

'But he didn't know he was slagging off my business. He was just citing an example.'

'You didn't tell him?'

Miriam shook her head and dumped the pizza back on the table.

'How could I? Oh, Rose, what have I done?'

Rose peered at her. 'Oh girl, you got it bad. There's better out there for you. Forget the opinionated dude.'

'But there isn't, and he wasn't. He's the first man I've connected with since, well, you know...and he ordered dessert first.'

'No way.' Rose's voice softened.

'He did.' Her stomach fizzed at the memory. How their eyes had met in surprise when they both asked for the dessert menu first.

Sleep was not an option. The horrified look on Jerry's face loomed large in her head, and giant bacteria waving flags with murderer written on them. These were followed by red bills, and sleeping rough on the streets. She threw off the bedclothes, grabbed a coffee, switched on her computer, and trawled through everything she could find on cleaning products and bacteria.

After eliminating hype and adverts, she came across a college website which shocked her brain awake. There were more bacteria cells than human cells in the body? What? Most bacteria are good, and over cleaning with strong chemicals can kill the microbes that fight off the harmful ones. Her knee bounced up and down so fast she ended up with cramp in her calf muscle.

Her work was doing more harm than good, but she needed her job. It had taken years to build up her client list. She paced the room.

'You're buzzing, girl. I'll have whatever you had for breakfast,' Rose said with bleary eyes and a yawn. 'Wait. Did you even go to bed?'

'No,' Miriam flicked on the kettle. 'You'll never believe what I've found out, and it's all because of Jerry.'

'Oh, Mirri babes. He's a bad guy, after all? Men are not worth crying over.'

'No. Not about him.' Although she'd been tempted. 'Those super strong "kills ninety-nine percent of germs" chemicals I use are doing more harm than good. I'm probably making my clients sick, and me too. All those migraines I get could be my fault. And I must tell them. My clients.' She slumped into the chair, resting her forehead on her hands. 'But then I won't have a job, and I'll be on the streets.'

'Too much caffeine and not enough zeds have addled your brain, love,' Rose said, and patted her on the shoulder. 'I'll make you a camomile tea and you reschedule your appointments for today and rest.'

'No, I can't.' Miriam groaned. 'If I tell my clients, they won't want me, and if I don't, I'm harming them. Oh, Ms Winter's asthma? What if it's my fault?' Her chest tightened and she couldn't breathe. Karma?

'And they say I'm the drama queen,' Rose muttered, and handed Miriam a cup of tea. 'Go to work, finish the week, rest on the weekend. I'm sorry I won't be here. But don't you do anything rash, girl. Promise.'

Miriam promised.

She spent the weekend experimenting with lemons, limes, white vinegar, surgical spirit, baking soda, tea tree essential oil, peppermint essential oil, Castile soap, a rosemary plant and olive oil. By Monday her body ached, but the flat was clean despite a slight lingering vinegar smell, and she had several bottles of natural cleaning products ready to fill her car.

She was sticking on the last label when Rose slammed through the front door.

'Damn it, girl, you didn't have a dirty weekend, that's for sure,' Rose said. 'Cleaning on your days off is a sign of something seriously wrong. We need to talk, but I've only time for a shower before work. Later, babes, it's a must.' She glared until Miriam nodded.

Rose vanished into the bathroom and Miriam smiled at her exclamations. The white vinegar and tea tree oil mix had dissolved the ever-growing mould around the shower base and window, with a little elbow grease thrown in. And it smelt fresh rather than chemical.

As Miriam's car spluttered its morning protest, she was still pondering what to tell her clients. Her business 'The SUPER STRONG CLEANER' - guaranteed to remove ninety-nine percent of all bacteria and one hundred percent of grime—was now a lie. Homemade cleaners would only eliminate the bad bacteria, leaving the good ones to live happily ever after.

Should she use the new cleaning products and see what her clients said? Could she cope with making them rather than ordering online? It was much cheaper, but time consuming. Although, once she'd perfected the recipes, it would be quicker, and they'd last longer if she didn't clean as much. What else did she have to do with her time? Dating was out. Jerry's face filled her head, and she wanted to cry. She was a bacteria killer, destroying the ecosystem one evil cleaning product at a time.

A horn blared, and she flinched. The light was green. She almost stalled the car in her haste to move. Damn the man for getting in her head, and not in her knickers. She blushed. What was wrong with her? She had to stop thinking about him. He'd probably looked her up and was even more disgusted with her.

'But I didn't know,' she said, but then shook her head. Ignorance was not an excuse.

Miriam parked in time to see her first client strapping her third child into the car. The youngest was screaming and scratching her arms, the poor kid had terrible eczema. There was no opportunity to talk to the frantic mum about using a different cleaning product, but when Miriam entered the house, she stared at the work surfaces. Should she use the new stuff without asking? Was it her fault the child had eczema? Or was she blowing this all out of proportion because her libido had awakened like a volcano, as Rose said?

Miriam clung to the kitchen island and made her choice. She couldn't risk harming a child. She'd use the new products in all her client's homes, but say nothing, and see what happened. And after a month, she'd send a letter to explain what she was now doing, and how she was going to change her business name and slogan, and then she would probably be signing on for universal credit.

She was right, her clients were furious she'd not informed them before changing her products. Letters condemned her as a fraud, misleading advertisement, a hippy, jumping on the green bandwagon, using them as an experiment, and betraying their trust. Some refused to pay her for the last month as they didn't want any germs growing in their house, thank you very much.

Only two clients kept her as their cleaner. Two. Her most demanding, who claimed she preferred the smell of the new products and whose asthma had lessened over the month, and the hurried mum, who said her daughter's eczema had calmed down. She'd invited Miriam to come to the mother and toddler group as many of the mums worried about the rise in asthma, eczema, and tummy bugs in their children despite keeping surfaces clean with anti-bacteria products.

Two clients, and both had listened to her advice. They only wanted her once a fortnight.

'Girl, you're screwed,' Rose had said when she'd told her. 'I can cover your share of the rent this month, hon. Give you time to see sense.'

How was she going to pay the bills? At least she had time to design her new business name and slogan, but what should she do with the chemicals stored in boxes in her bedroom? The company didn't do refunds, and she didn't know how to dispose of them.

'Sell 'em on eBay, girl. That's the easiest way,' Rose said, but Miriam's conscience wouldn't let her.

'It's money you need, love,' Rose said with a shake of her head. 'I'll sell them for you.'

'No, it's the same thing. Now I know what it does, I can't.'

Rose patted her shoulder and left for work.

Work. Miriam sighed. At least she wasn't spending much on fuel or cleaning products. She had plenty of ingredients left to make more and had a good idea of which worked best.

She flicked through the local paper, looking for people wanting a cleaner. There were several, but after a closer look at their numbers, she blinked away tears. They were her old customers. A wave of despair and regret turned into fierce anger. Miriam threw the paper in the bin.

'Stupid woman. Why did you listen to a man and destroy your perfectly good business?' Although it wasn't a good business, just one that paid the bills. She grabbed the paper back out of the bin and tucked it in to her cleaning basket. It was brilliant for cleaning windows, and better for the environment. Man-made cloths leaked tiny plastic fibres. She froze.

'Oh, no. Rose is right. I've turned into an eco-nerd.' Tears plopped onto the table. Why was it so hard to do the right thing? Or find the right man? Wait. Had she jeopardised her business for a man? She shook her head. No, she was doing this because it was important and felt right, and what was wrong with being an eco-nerd anyway? She could share her knowledge at the toddler group and maybe get more clients, but she wasn't an expert and what if their children got sick?

She stared at her cleaning basket, which was prettier than a plastic box, and the word "mental" stared back from an advert on the back page of the newspaper.

'That sums me up.' She pulled the paper back out.

'Oh. Environmental Answers. Ha. Let's see if you can answer my list of questions.' She picked up her phone and tapped in the number.

'Environmental Answers. Zara here. How may I help you?'

Fifteen minutes later the woman had convinced Miriam to meet with their environmental projects manager, despite her protest that her problem was about her job, not a community project, and one week later, Miriam was walking into town through the park, with a folder full of research and ideas. It was so pretty, and the fresh air eased her mounting panic.

She stopped. When was the last time she had sat on the grass and read a book, or had a picnic? She listened to the birdsong and the buzz of insects. How could she ever use strong chemicals again? This was the right choice, even if she became homeless.

The Environmental Answers offices were above a café in a side street and the scent of coffee was tempting, but she couldn't waste a penny. She swigged cold water from her flask, wiped her sweaty hands on her dress, and entered. She felt like an imposter, but before she could run away, 'please call me Zara' said,

'You must be Miriam. You can go straight in.'

Miriam walked through the open door and froze.

Jerry stood. His face mirrored her surprise.

'Miriam?'

'Oh, I think this is a mistake,' she stepped back and bashed her elbow on the door frame. 'Ouch, ow.' She blinked away tears. What a twit she was. 'I'll leave, and I'm sorry to waste your time. It was such a great night, and I spoilt it and after I looked everything up, and... sorry.' Shut up, brain. She turned to leave, but Jerry was closing the door and taking her arm, not the one that throbbed, and leading her to a comfy chair.

'Sit down. Elbows hurt like hell. Can I get you something, ice maybe?'

She shook her head.

'I'm fine.'

He sat in the chair opposite but didn't meet her eyes.

'I guess you're here to shout at me,' he said. 'Go ahead. I deserve it. Slagging off your company, although I didn't know it was yours until the next day. I was so embarrassed, and the look on your face. I should have called, but I knew you'd never want to see me again.' He scratched his neck.

Miriam stared. Was he blushing?

'But I did,' she said, and it was her turn to blush. 'I didn't think you'd want to see me. You were horrified when I said I was a cleaner.'

'No, I was horrified I'd insulted you.'

His mouth twitched and within seconds, they were both laughing, although Miriam didn't know why. Her heart thumped louder than a steam train when, somehow, they ended up holding hands.

'Then why are you here, Miriam? Zara said something about mothers and toddler talks, but...?'

He pulled his hand away, raised his eyebrows and looked at her, melting away any coherent thought she had.

'Um, yes, sort of.' She fumbled in her bag for her folder. 'I did some research and changed my products to natural ones. Now I don't have a business, but I do have lots of nasty chemicals I can't dispose of. I can't pay my rent, but I can't sell the stuff. One of my clients wants me to talk to mums about microbes, but what if I say the wrong thing?' Her hands shook and all the pages fluttered out of the folder.

Miriam grabbed the nearest sheets.

'Stop,' Jerry said, picking one up and reading, 'Gentle Green Cleaner–a healthier clean home. Wait, you risked your business because of me?'

'For the environment,' she said. 'But mostly for you.' She groaned. 'Did I say that out loud?'

'You did.' He grinned. 'Shall we discuss your ideas? Zara thinks they have potential for a grant, and after we could try that new desert café, if you'd like?'

Germ Counselling

by Jamie Mollart

The room is too hot.

Jess is worrying about how this makes it a breeding room for germs.

Tim is trying to remember if he put on any deodorant as he feels a light trickle of sweat make its way out of his armpit.

Alexia is oblivious to the temperature. It's her room, so it's set to where she feels comfortable. No one has ever mentioned the fact that it's too hot, but then the people who come in here are normally broken in one way or another and often lack the confidence to confront the person who is supposed to help them. That or they consider it to be part of the process: a hot therapy or something. Alexia's husband has long since stopped noticing the fact that their house is equally tropical, puts it down to some African blood in her somewhere, which he says explains the amazing corkscrew hair as well. She gesticulates at a sofa.

Jess looks at it, calculations powering through her head, eventually deciding she's got to take the risk and sits down, trying not to imagine the explosion of microbes and dust mites and fuck knows what else erupting out of the leather as it succumbs to her weight.

Tim sees all this happening in her head and wants to shake her, worries that Alexia sees it too and that she'll take offense and they'll start off on the wrong foot and that means it won't work and they'll be stuck like this in perpetuity, and that can't happen.

Alexia hasn't noticed it, because although she's read the long email which Tim sent her, she has put that at the back of her mind, at least for now. She's a believer in instinct, and these moments, when the clients first come into her space, are like gold dust for her intuition. The way they are with each other, the way they interact, the way they sit, the first words they say, who talks first - all of this builds up her tapestry of understanding.

So instead of noticing Jess's discomfort and Tim's reciprocal discomfort, she notices the tension in their bodies and the gap between them and the clenched teeth and she wants to whistle and say 'whooooo, this is going to be a tough one.'

But she's a consummate professional, so she smiles a smile which is all teeth and welcome and understanding and she says 'hi, both, my name is Alexia, and it's my job to try to help you with whatever it is you want to talk about today.'

Tim looks at Jess, Jess looks at Tim. Then they both start to talk at the same time. Alexia raises a hand to slow them down.

'I can't live like this anymore,' says Tim.

'He's becoming impossible to live with,' says Jess at the same time.

They make a nervous laugh together as if they've just interrupted each other as they are ordering coffee, not telling a stranger they're paying to listen to them, that they're not happy in their lives.

'Okay,' says Alexia, 'well, we agree on this, which believe it or not is a starting point. If you both agree you aren't happy with the current situation and you're both here, then you're both agreeing that you want to make a change. So, Tim, let's start with you. Can you tell me why you're here?'

'She's got a terrible temper.'

Two weeks earlier - it's late; the dark evening is trying to work its way into the house through the gaps in the curtains, the invasive damp of an English evening. Tim is cold, he is already wearing a jumper, but it's not working, the fingers of cold are finding their way through the gaps on the knit. He assesses Jess. She's just wearing a t-shirt. Maybe he's coming down with something. No. She's like a radiator half the time. She just doesn't ever seem affected by the cold.

'I'm going to make a fire,' Tim says.

She grunts a reply. She's on her phone and watching True Detective at the same time, he's way down on her sensory priority list.

He opens the front of the log burner and as he does so a draft from the chimney picks up the ash and swirls it out of the burner and across the lounge like the aftermath of a bomb. That attracts her attention alright.

'What are you doing?' she's screaming, her voice right on the knife edge of hysteria.

'Making a fire,' he replies.

She looks at him like he's insane, points at his shoes, her mouth opening and shutting.

'What now?'

'Have you seen the bottom of your shoes?'

He shrugs. He hadn't. He tends not to think too much about his shoes. They're just things on his feet to keep them warm and dry. He plonks himself down on the hearth amongst the ash and turns one of his feet upwards to see the bottom.

'Dirt,' he says.

She tuts.

'What?' he says, while thinking, why can't I keep my mouth shut? Why am I goading her?

'I spent hours cleaning this floor today. Fucking hours.'

He looks at it and shrugs again, and she flips her lid. He's not even listening to the words, it's just a barrage of noise. He ignores her and starts sweeping up the ash. He catches the end of an expletive laden sentence and before he can stop himself has shouted back at her, 'it's just a bit of dirt Jess.'

She shoves him with her palm and he topples backwards from his haunches and is left perched on the stone hearth as she storms from the room.

Alexia listens to the story, watches the scowl on Jess's face as he talks, takes in the fact that she doesn't argue with him, just stares at him as if he's talking a foreign language. When he finishes, they sit in silence while Alexia writes some notes on her pad. The silence is deliberate. She wants to see how they interact. The answer is they don't. Eventually Alexia takes pity on them and says, 'thank you for sharing Tim. Jess, have you got anything you'd like to talk about?'

Jess looks at Alexia under lidded eyes, seems to consider things for a moment, then looks at Tim as if weighing up whether she wants to, then leans forward and rests her palms on her knees.

'He's lazy and disrespectful.'

'Now, hang on a minute...' starts Tim, but Alexia stops him with a raised palm.

The kitchen is a sacred space. Jess likes it just so. When she's in another room, she can sense it. If things are wrong, she feels it like a throb under the ambient noise of the house, it gnaws at her.

Today, over her lunch hour she cleaned it. The day has been draining. She's dealing with a terrible case, it's haunting her, but she can't share details with Tim, so instead she seeks relief in the cleaning of things. She took out all the pots and pans. Washed each of them in water as near to 90 degrees as she could get it without burning herself.

There's a satisfaction in it, albeit a temporary one, and as soon as she sits back down, basking in a sense of peace, she instantly begins to worry about the high traffic area of the kitchen.

This pathway from the lounge to the fridge is the most direct line between the two areas and is so used that in the right light she can see the buffed, polished strip of carpet and lino. The hundreds of times that feet have traipsed over it, the thousands of grubby footsteps treading the outside in and then spreading it over the house. It gnaws at her. She's supposed to get this report in by the end of the day, but it's impossible, the path of grime is glowing in her peripheral and won't go away until she does something about it. She gives in. Gets out a thick brush and works her way back and forth across the carpet three, then four, then five times. Then she gets out the hoover and goes over it in both directions of travel, then each way across the grain, then does it all again just to be sure.

Mostly satisfied, she moves into the kitchen and on her hands and knees scrubs at the floor with Dettol, then again with bleach, then a multi-surface cleaner. By the time she's done, her hands are red and the house smells like a hospital. She closes that thought down. Hospitals aren't clean. Hospitals are full of dirt and germs and antibiotic resistant drugs and sepsis.

Tim is utterly oblivious. Jess is working at the dining room table when he comes in.

'Hi honey,' she calls out to him, but he's talking to himself, no he's talking to someone on the phone, white earphones wedged into his ears, either way he doesn't acknowledge her. He kicks his shoes off in the middle of the kitchen, one of them flopping onto their side and displaying its tread to her, complete with mud and leaves wedged in the grooves. She feels herself prickle but manages not to say anything. He drops his bag on the floor next to the kitchen table.

Tim is getting annoyed. Maybe it's the passive aggressive nature of the questions, maybe it's the way Jess is coldly throwing him under the bus, maybe it's all of the above, but he can feel anger rising in him. He promised himself that he would embrace the process going into this, that his marriage is worth saving, gazing at the happiness in their wedding photos to motivate himself. It worked, if only by contrast. The Jess in the pictures isn't the Jess he is sitting next to on a sagging sofa in an overheated office. The picture Jess was happy and fun and carefree. The picture Jess was spontaneous, exciting, and excitable. The sofa Jess is neurotic and angry and drains the life out of him. The sofa Jess is not the same person as the picture Jess, and he wants picture Jess back. He wants to be eloquent enough to explain this to both sofa Jess and this lady sitting opposite him with wild hair and an earnest expression.

Instead, he blurts out, 'I feel like I'm a rat in a cage.'

Both of them look at him shocked and he realises not only is that offensive, but it's also not what he meant.

He tries to correct himself but ends up stuttering a nonsensical sentence instead.

They're staring at him. This is what he means, this is what he was trying to get across.

'This is what I mean. The way you're looking at me. Like I'm an idiot or a problem. This is what it's like being at home. Nothing I do is right. I feel like I'm being stared at and judged all the time. I have to tiptoe around my own house.'

'That's interesting,' says Alexia, 'do you want to expand on that?'

'Do you know how hot it is in here?' he says, adjusting his collar.

'Is it?' says Alexia, looking genuinely perplexed.

'Roasting,' he says, 'really bad for the environment.'

He's aware he sounds petty, but it's a fact and he cares about it, so he doesn't apologise, instead pushing on.

'It's better if we all keep our heating below 19 degrees. Saves energy and lowers pollution.'

It's one of his bugbears. He's not an eco-warrior or anything, but if everybody did little things, it would make a big difference. Jess is the same. Everything needs to be washed at 90 degrees all the time. It pisses him off. It shrinks his shirts and the bed sheets stink of detergent all the time. She basically boils everything. She boils herself too. Hours in the shower, steam billowing out of the bathroom, until her skin is bright red, and she has to slather it with moisturiser to hide the fact that she's drying it out with shower gel.

He's taken to waiting until she's put the washing on, sneaking it and resetting it at 30 degrees. It gives him a sense of satisfaction. He's hardly stapling himself to a road in protest at carbon emissions, but it's something.

He looks at his knees as Alexia stands, walks over to the thermostat and lowers the temperature. When she returns, she glances at her notes, then says, 'you were telling us about how you feel like you have to tiptoe round your own house?'

He's eating his dinner. Jess ate hers earlier. She knew he was going to be late today, so she ate beforehand but didn't make enough for two and so he is eating a cheese and tomato ketchup sandwich leaning over the island. He's exhausted. A day of meeting after meeting; most of which he could have avoided, but the trend for growing invite lists that began in the pandemic hasn't gone away now the world is open again. His online diary is a patchwork of blocked out time. Of meetings with no agendas which would be no worse off if he didn't show, but that's not how it works. Your name is on the invite list, and you have to attend.

'I'm going to start refusing to attend them unless I get told before-hand why I've been invited and what is expected of me,' he says to Jess with a mouth half full of sandwich.

She doesn't reply, so he looks up at her, licking at the blob of ketchup lodged in the corner of his mouth.

She is glowering at him in disgust.

'What?' he asks.

She doesn't reply, instead just points at the corner of her mouth, turns on her heel and leaves the room.

'I know,' he shouts after her, then mutters, 'for fuck's sake' under his breath. Somewhere in the house, a door slams shut. His grip on the sandwich loosens and cheese and sauce falls onto the work surface.

'For fuck's sake,' he says louder this time and dumps the sandwich on the surface, trying to scoop the cheese back into the bread and dabbing at the sauce with his index finger before popping it into his mouth.

The cat flap goes, and their ginger tom jumps onto the island. Instinctively he puts his forearm under the cat's belly to scoop it off, but she's been a dick, so he lets the cat plonk itself down and feeds it a bit of cheese.

Tim's phone rings. He curses himself. He thought he'd put it on silent. Jess had asked him to turn it off, but there's stuff going on at work that he wants, needs to know about and he's angling for promotion so he needs to be visible on everything and it's wearing him down, but what can he do about it.

'Sorry,' he says to Alexia and then, sensing Jess's disapproving eyes on the side of his head, more forcibly, 'sorry.'

He shuts it down, trying not to notice that it's his boss's number on the screen. As he puts it away into his pocket, a sneeze blasts out of him before he can stop himself. He doesn't even get his arm up in time to cover it. He feels Jess tense against his leg. He mutters sorry again. Alexia reaches behind her and grabs a box of tissues and hands it to him. He takes one and dabs at his face. He's painfully aware that sneezing in public is even less socially acceptable than it used to be and says, 'sorry, it's not Covid, just a niggling cold I can't shift.'

'You're always ill,' says Jess.

'I'm not.'

'You are. I can't remember the last time you didn't have a cold.'

He thinks about it for a second and internally concedes she's probably right but doesn't want to admit it out loud.

'That's hardly fair,' he says instead.

'It's not fair or unfair, it's just the truth.'

'Bullshit,' he says, aware that the language represents an escalation.

'Don't swear at me,' says Jess.

'Don't make shit up about me then.'

'What? I just pointed out that you've had a cold forever. It's hardly important, is it?'

'You're constantly having a go at me. There's always something. It's got to be at least once an hour. So negative'

'You're the one who's negative.'

'Come off it.'

'You are. There's always a problem. So and so did this at work. So and so did that. Fuck so and so. It's constant. It wears me out. You're like this negative force that keeps picking at things.'

'You're kidding me right? You're the one that picks.'

Alexia leans back in her chair. She thinks she's getting somewhere with them but wants to see how this plays out, sure that somewhere in this petty name calling is the core problem.

'What are you talking about, Tim?' Jess asks.

He puts on a whiny voice and wiggles his head side to side in a mocking caricature of her as he says 'don't leave your bag there, don't leave your shoes there, I've just cleaned that, you're dropping crumbs, wash your hands before you touch that, don't dump that there. Sound familiar?'

It does. It sounds just like her, but she doesn't see a problem with it.

'It's like living with a child,' she says.

'It's like living with a mental person.'

They both slam back into the chair, expressions set, mouths sealed in tight lines. Alexia leaves them there for a second, then leans forward.

'Can we try something?' she asks.

They're spiky on the sofa. Neither of them want to reply. Alexia ignores them, goes to her desk, and pulls out a pad and a couple of pens. She tears out a couple of pages and lays them on the coffee table before them and drops a pen on each.

Tim picks the pen up and immediately pops it in his mouth and contemplatively starts chewing it. Jess takes out a small bottle of sanitising gel, squeezes some into her hand, and slathers it over the pen.

'It's her thing,' says Tim in an apologetic tone, and then when Jess glowers at him wonders why he can't stop himself from spilling his mind unfiltered from his mouth.

'I want you to both draw me something. If you can avoid looking at what the other one is drawing, that would be better.'

Jess picks up the paper and pen and goes over to the bookcase, using the top of it to rest the paper on.

'Can you both draw me some bacteria?'

'Really?' asks Jess.

'Humour me.'

Tim quickly scribbles something on the paper and then waits, still chewing his pen while Jess produces what will no doubt be a fucking masterpiece.

Eventually she folds the paper in half and takes it back to Alexia, so he hands his over too.

'Thank you,' says Alexia, then, 'Tim, can I ask you about your family?'

'Pretty normal really. Dad was an accountant, Mum worked in HR. I had a fairly standard suburban upbringing, I think. No big dramas, nothing horrendous, but nothing too momentous either.'

'Jess?'

Even at his most obstreperous and mid argument, Tim fastidiously avoids any mention of her family.

Jess remembers the kitchen of their family home most of all. It was white and tiled and wasn't touched in any way by the family that lived in it. There were no pictures of the kids or artwork stuck on a fridge. Not because the parents weren't proud of their children, this was a house built on love even it if was the sort from a Victorian novel, but because the kitchen was a space for her mother and her mother, a paediatric nurse liked things to be clean and tidy and orderly.

This particular morning, things weren't orderly.

Jess's teenage brother is controlled primarily by his hormones and a bundle of spots and sulking and outbursts. The family are due to travel to the coast to stay with an Aunt whose name Jess can't remember, just an amorphous shape made of high-necked dresses, bouffont hair and a small dog that yaps at Jess's ankles whenever she goes near it. The dog's name was Princess.

The small TV on the work surface, a ridiculous luxury that she never understood her mother allowing, is playing an advert for some disinfectant or other, promising to clear 99.9% of all bacteria, and her father, a GP so austere that even his friends refer to him as Dr Blake, appears in the kitchen doorway.

'Utter twaddle,' he scoffs.

Her mother refuses to bite, trying to usher her brother to finish his breakfast and get dressed, so her father continues at a louder volume. Jess is actually interested. She isn't close to her father, but she respects him to a degree that verges on hero worship.

'Firstly, that stuff is tested in a laboratory, so to say it kills 99.9% of bacteria in a petri dish is one thing, to do it in a house is another.'

'James, will you please eat your breakfast, we should have left 10 minutes ago, we're going to get caught in the traffic, we said we'd be there by 12, and your aunt has booked us a table,' her mother's voice is sharp with stress and anxiety.

James barely registers. Just carries on staring at his Weetabix through the shield of his curtain hair and pushing the claggy mixture around the bowl.

'Secondly, bacteria isn't bad. We need it in our body. It's a gross misinterpretation of the facts to suggest that killing all bacteria is a good thing.'

'James, I'm going to give you to the count of ten to finish that cereal.'

He looks up under a furrowed brow and snarls 'or what?'

Her mother looks at her father for help, but he's either not listening or choosing to ignore her.

'It's a marketing myth to sell more units of disinfectant. It's not based on medical thinking at all. It's idiotic. We're mostly bacteria.

They've evolved with us, they're integral to us. You try and kill them, and you kill yourself.'

'James, seriously, we need to go. Everyone is ready apart from you.'

James ignores her.

'James,' her voice is shrill now, she's stabbing at the air in front of him with her index finger. He reaches up and bats it away. She squeals a noise that is somewhere between incredulous and angry and turns to her husband.

'Are you going to let him treat me like that?'

'James, don't treat your mother like that.'

'Whatever.'

Her father moves so quickly it shocks all of them. He's generally a calm man. A measured man. Now though, one minute he is in the doorway, the next he is at the table. He snatches up the bowl of cereal and launches it at the wall where it explodes like a blood splatter on the tiles. Then he is at James's level, his voice calm and sinister, and he says in a perfectly level tone, 'if you're not in the bloody car in five minutes I'll drag you down the drive myself.'

The shock on James's face would be comic if it wasn't so childlike and genuine. He looks like he's going to cry. He pushes the chair back and leaves the room. Their father follows him, picks up the suitcases from the hall and begins loading the car. Jess and her mother begin to tidy up the mess. When her father returns, Jess is dabbing at the mess on the wall with a sponge.

'Leave that, he can do it,' her father says.

But James doesn't clean it up. He takes longer than five minutes and her fathers face is turning redder by the second, screaming up the stairs at James, who appears with his bags, firmly back into sullen teenager mode, and the argument continues through the door, which is slammed behind them.

They fight down the drive as Jess and her mother follow them at enough of a distance to not be directly involved.

They fight as they climb into the car amongst slammed doors and the angry clunk of seatbelts.

They're still fighting as they join the main road and it's still going as her father turns over his shoulder to remonstrate his son, as the car crosses the white lines in the centre of the road and slams into a transit van coming the other way. Jess feels the jolt as a seismic force. Their world lifts and shifts, full of noise and broken glass, and then she passes out.

Days later when she is released from hospital, picked up by her grandmother as the rest of her family cool in the morgue, she returns to an empty home, where she finds the remains of the Weetabix rotted into a gag inducing graffiti mural across the kitchen wall, and a thought insinuates itself into her head – if I'd have cleaned this then they wouldn't have died.

Jess has never told Tim this story before. It has always felt too personal, too tragic to share the details of. He knew her family died in a car crash and that's all. Here now, as she fingers the scar under her right eye caused by the accident, she feels horribly exposed. Alexia leans forward and then, asking permission with her eyes, gently squeezes her knee with an expression which is somewhere between gratitude and understanding.

'Right,' she says, 'shall we look at your drawings?'

She unfurls the paper onto the table in front of them and leans back. A low whistle escaping her mouth.

It's almost comical how different they are.

Tim's drawing of bacteria is a chirpy little fella all smiley mouth and googly eyes. It's eyebrows arch at quizzical angles and the whole thing has the air of a drunken Mr Men drawing.

Jess's on the other hand, is born of nightmares. Jagged lines. Spikes and snarling spines promising death and a painful one at that.

They couldn't have drawn two more contrasting images if that had been the brief.

Alexia folds her arms across her chest, seemingly satisfied, as this has resolved something or cemented a thought in her mind.

'Well done both of you,' she says, 'That can't have been easy for you.'

Tim makes a scoff in his throat and then tries to hide it with a cough, then tries to swallow that because he's worried they'll equate it with the earlier sneeze.

'Really?' says Jess, suppressing an urge to punch Tim hard in the side of his head.

'Really.'

'How so?' asks Tim, feeling more annoyed with Jess than when he came in, not less.

'I'm going to ask you a question, Jess, and I want you to know it comes from a place of love with no accusation and no judgement.'

It's a statement, not a question, but is said in such a way that Jess understands she needs to reply before Alexia will continue.

'Okay,' she says, masking the trepidation in her voice.

'Have you ever been assessed for obsessive cleaning?'

'What?' Jess laugh says this is ridiculous, but even as the laugh dies, something begins to click into place in her head.

'I'm not saying there's not issues here that we need to talk about, not least the fact that you're struggling to talk to each other, but I think it's more pressing that we look at getting Jess help.'

Jess's mouth is wide open and flapping as her brain tries to catch up.

'How long have you struggled with the idea of bacteria and germs?'

Jess thinks about it and realises she's right and that it wasn't always this way. Something sinks inside her and Alexia sees it happen, takes the tissues from Tim's lap in time to catch the tears that start to flow. Jess's shoulders drop, her head follows, a tissue goes to her face and her whole body is wracked with silent sobs.

It makes sense now. She feels foolish that she's not seen it before. Like every other person in the world, she always assumed she was the normal one and everyone else looked out through the lens of lunacy.

Tim looks at Jess. Then he looks at Alexia, who nods at him.

He puts his arm around her shoulders and pulls her into him. 'Shit Jess, why didn't you say anything? Like I knew you liked things clean, but I didn't think you had OCD.'

'Ah, we don't know that,' says Alexia, 'we need to work with Jess to assess that, but I can tell you right now that she has a compulsion to clean which is unhealthy and we need to look at ways to help her. It's my professional opinion that if we do that, the rest of the issues you are facing will be relatively simple. Are you up for taking that journey with me, Jess?'

Jess came here ready to go on a journey. She was already sold on the idea. It's just a different journey to the one she expected.

'Yes,' her voice is a whisper.

'Jess,' says Tim into her hair, and she's photo Jess again, the smell of disinfectant previously a quirk, now something that he wants to protect her from.

Jess allows herself to fold into his body and for the first time in ages feels something like hope.

The Smell of Success

by Catherine Kerr

I don't want to be forgiven. Remember that, when you read the rest of this. *I don't want to be forgiven*.

(I don't deserve to be.)

***

It started in October, just as the world was turning away from the sun and the trees had donned cloaks of gold and amber-bronze. I was hurrying to work, hot chocolate clutched in one hand and a too-heavy briefcase dragging down the other. The hand holding my hot drink was the only part of me that was warm. The wind was trying to snatch my hat and playing tag with my scarf, and all I cared about was getting indoors.

The bus wasn't indoors, precisely, but it was better than the howling wind, which made it feel like I was trapped inside a fridge.

Hunched in my seat, it took me several moments to notice the poster – but when I did, my attention was riveted.

NOW HIRING! It declared in big bold letters. The splash of red was a shocking snap of colour against the grey-blue monotone of the bus.

It seemed harmless. I'm sure that poster didn't bring about calamity for any other passenger riding the bus that day. But it snagged my attention, and as I read more, I thought, almost hopefully, *I could do that*.

And that's how it started.

~~~

"What qualifies you for this job?" the woman asked. The man beside her had been silent for almost the entirety of the interview, watching me with crossed arms, and it was making me nervous.

I babbled about my qualifications, my university degree, my confidence and great communication skills. I'm sure the rambling nature of my answer undermined everything I was saying. Interviews truly are their own special sort of bulbous wart.

"Anything else?" the woman asked blandly, after I'd warbled long enough that I'd started to crumble like a biscuit. I'm sure they thought I had about as much substance as one.

"I– ah, um–" I stammered – and then, in a fit of desperation, I blurted out, "I'm very keen! I'll – I'll do anything!"

The man finally sat up.

He liked that.

Stupidly, I felt good about that. I was proud of myself for finally saying the right thing.

I never really stopped to think about what it meant, that he'd only approved once I'd said I'd do *anything*.

But, well… it's not like I *really* meant it. And it's not like he'd expect me to.

~~~

"I want ideas, and I want them now," Richard said. I was forty-three minutes into my new job, and I'd learned a lot about Richard in that time. Frankly, I was hoping that I'd be able to keep up.

"We go for the obvious market, target mothers, play the guilt card," Sarah said.

"Get a doctor in a TV ad talking about how the plague spread, or something. Measles is infectious, right? Or... I dunno, chickenpox? Morton and co. tried to go the STD route and failed horribly, *obviously*. Idiots. As if people want *clean* sex!"

"I like it," Kirk said, nodding approvingly and scribbling a note. "That way, we can plant subtle doubts – if I'm not clean enough, will I make my kids sick?"

"Oh yeah, worried mums everywhere will eat that right up," Sarah agreed.

"Dads are a dead market – half of them don't even wash their hands, they're not going to buy cleaning products," Alina said with a snort. "The best we can do is try to convince them to clean their car or buy a car air freshener."

"Or use military-sounding names like Assassinate or Killemkwik," said Kirk.

Sarah hummed doubtfully. "We could try the kid angle on them too? An ad on Father's Day, thanking dads for always keeping us safe? Have a sick kid who gets better thanks to the love and care from their father? Who just so happens to use antibacterial wipes?"

Kirk scoffed. "Have you *heard* of Twitter? The feminists would put that one in the ground in the first ten hours. Are you saying women can't keep their kids safe? What about the kids who don't have dads? And–"

"Alright, alright, it was just an idea," Sarah said irritably.

"A sale never fails," Alina said, as if reciting something from the gospel of capitalism. "We get the supermarkets to run a three for two deal, or sell the products in packs of two... Maybe say we're doing it for the environment to save packaging?"

"The plastic wrapping defeats the purpose of *oh goodness, I just love the planet so much*," Sarah said drily.

Alina blinked at her. "So?" She cocked an eyebrow. "Everyone's an idiot. Stick a cartoon planet on there and people will snatch it up to feel better about themselves. Yes, I bought this nice bottle of bleach, I'm an eco-hero, go me."

"I still think the mums are the best angle," Kirk said. "Our way in is the kids. They fall for it every time. All we have to do is imply that they're bad mums if they're not protecting their kids from germs – I mean, just think about all that dirt they play around in! Who knows what's been in your lawn? Goodness, we'll just have to offer you some of our wipes right away, ma'am..."

I cleared my throat nervously.

The whole room turned to me.

"There's another market I think you could target," I began, and then cleared my throat again. Say it. Just say it.

"Yes?" Kirk asked. Richard was watching me.

Now is your chance.

"Teenagers," I stated.

Kirk gave me a doubtful look.

"Teenagers are perhaps the filthiest species on the entire planet," Sarah said flatly.

I laughed anxiously and took a deep breath. "Yes, but, well... teenage girls are more insecure than ever. So... so we tell them they smell. We tell them they've got dry, dull hair and spotty, oily skin and they'll never get a guy unless they buy our specially formulated products, scientifically proven to work wonders on all of their problems."

The room blinked at me.

"The mums are already buying cleaning products," I continued when no one interrupted me. "It's an over-saturated market, and mums tend to limit their purchases, because they're old enough to understand money, and they have bills to pay. Teenagers don't, and they're fantastic impulse buyers. You don't even need a doctor to convince them – just an influencer on TikTok or Instagram, and then they'll convince themselves. Even better, they'll convince their friends, too. And once you've got them, you've got them for life."

Richard smiled.

"Go on," he said, and I did.

It was a rush, knowing that I could keep up.

~~~

The company launched a chain of new products, all specifically targeting teenage girls and young women – sprays, lotions, wipes, shampoos and conditioners... you name it, we were selling it. Sarah had the great idea of creating cutesy little air fresheners with artsy motivational quotes, and they sold out in a fortnight.

Richard was happy, so we were happy.

Then the call came.

"Somebody pull up the news headlines!" Richard barked, and soon we were all gathered around Kirk's computer.

CANCER IN A CAN? cried the headline.

"It's a hit piece on formaldehyde," Sarah said, after a tense moment of skim reading.

"Have we been named?" Richard demanded.

There was another horrible pause.

"No," Sarah said, and we all breathed a sigh of relief.

"Right, scrap the formaldehyde. We're going to have to use something else in our products," Richard announced. "And we need to change the formulas *now*, before the papers catch wind of this. We do *not* want this bad press!"

By the end of the week, our adorable little "Stay happy!" air fresheners were using terpenes instead. Terpenes such as limonene occurred naturally in the air and had a citrusy smell. We glossed over the fact it reacts with ozone in the air to form formaldehyde. Anyway on its own, it was well below dangerous levels - outdoors anyway. We didn't ask ourselves how it contributed to the combined toxic load from chemicals in shampoos, cosmetics, and other cleaning products.

"We can gloss over the use of terpenes by promoting our products as formaldehyde free," Alina said. "And nothing has even been definitively proven about terpenes, anyway. These days, people's version of research is TikTok and Twitter. We can use that to our advantage, and run a campaign about how we're Here for Health, or something."

I thought she was clever.

Ha. I actually thought she was clever.

None of us were. We were just greedy and blind.

(Or maybe we were too clever for our own good.)

Our campaign targeting teenagers worked beautifully – so beautifully that I got a promotion and a pay raise.

I was very happy.

Kirk had given me one of their new designs for the car air fresheners: a little sun wearing shades, with "Smells like Success!" in bright orange across the bottom. I thought it was cheery.

I binned it, obviously. It had terpenes in it.

Who'd want to be breathing in *that*?

~~~

My sister called, begging for babysitting. She had a doctor's appointment she couldn't miss, and two wailing kids that weren't interested in being stuck in the car for an hour.

I related to the plight. Not my sister's – no, I hadn't made the mistake of having kids yet. Rather, I remembered all too well the feeling of my brains slowly melting out my ears as I died of boredom, as yet another kid stuck somewhere with nothing exciting whilst the adults did Adult Things.

We went for ice cream and ran around the park and generally made a mess of ourselves. It was fantastic.

And then my sister returned, and as she pulled her car up to the kerb, I noticed something that made my blood run colder than October wind.

Hanging from the rear-view mirror in my sister's car was a very familiar little cartoon sun.

I didn't think we were half so clever, then.

"Have the kids washed their hands?" my sister asked, looking nervously at where my nephew had gotten a small grass stain on his knee, and my niece had managed to dribble vanilla ice cream on the cuff of her shirt. "Should I get a wipe?"

"What? Yes, of course they did, why would you...?" I began, confused, and then I trailed off.

Everyone's an idiot, I could hear Alina saying clearly in my head.

It had never quite occurred to me that *everyone* included *my sister*.

My *sister*.

I turned back to my niece, who was grinning up at me like I'd hung every star in every constellation just to see her smile.

Our way in is the kids.

"Thanks for taking such good care of them," my sister said gratefully, and gave me her own starlit smile, and I felt wintry to my core.

Because I hadn't taken care of them at all, had I?

Teenage girls are more insecure than ever, my own voice echoed back at me.

I couldn't stop staring at my niece. She was only ten.

But she wouldn't stay ten forever.

I wanted to tell her, suddenly, that she didn't need to watch out for the monster under the bed – just the carcinogens in her mum's laundry detergent.

...And the monster in her family that had convinced the world they were safe.

"Alice," I said abruptly. "Alice, bin the air freshener. And – and what cleaning products do you use?"

My sister blinked at me, utterly taken aback. Utterly confused.

Utterly innocent.

"What?" she asked, baffled, and I wondered how to tell her without scaring her.

I was already scared.

What Lives in the Ice

by Eleanor Rycroft

It was Thursday night in the library. We'd sat on saggy blue-bloated chairs in a circle and talked about "our problems" for a whole hour, the words hushed, drifting to the brink of our group before they were eaten up by metal shelves and books in plastic wrapping. Now, in a mistaken attempt at good cheer, the organisers had wheeled out a drinks cart. We were encouraged to mingle. Perhaps they thought this would be a reward.

The canny survivors had already made for the door, shedding excuses with easy practice. I hadn't been quick enough. Foolishly tempted by own-brand lemonade and sad sausage rolls, I'd been cornered by Pete in front of Memoirs and Biographies. Poor Pete. His son had died of leukaemia. I felt I ought to like him more than I did.

"I thought that was really brave," Pete said earnestly. Everything he did was earnest. "Opening up like that. It can be really hard to be honest about life after loss, but you said it so well."

Sometimes, I pictured my tolerance like an elastic band. I could stretch it so far, talk about It so much, and then I needed a break to loosen off the tension. Right now, after an hour and a day and eight long months, I could feel myself creaking under the strain. Those little tears were appearing in the edge of the rubber, saw-toothed gaps, bitter dried-out cracks. The world felt suddenly cold.

"Sorry, Pete," I said. "I really need to nip to the bathroom."

"Oh, of course, of course," he was saying, but I was already leaving, abandoning my plastic cup of fizz on the information desk.

I really did go to the bathroom. I sat in there for a while, deciding whether to use this as my chance to bolt. It really was a simple exercise in old-fashioned scales: this side weighs this much, the other... Mental arithmetic. I'd gotten quite good at it since It happened. I decided, on balance, to stay, but to hide. This was an adequate compromise.

I'd also gotten quite good at hiding. Like a wraith in the night, I silently reclaimed my lemonade and glided towards Women's Fiction. I knew there was another secret seat there, tucked between the shelves for F and the shelves for J. When I made it, I breathed a sigh of relief.

I'd visited this seat many times before. It was the best spot in the library; away from main traffic, hidden from the central gathering space. There were actually two chairs here, set at companionable angles, a low table between them. Perhaps by design, a poster had been tacked to the end of the J shelf. It was a picture of a green meadow beneath a blue sky. In the sky, words had been written in the clouds: you are not alone. I looked at that poster quite a lot when I squirreled myself away here and pondered the irony.

"You really aren't alone, you know."

I looked up like I'd been caught, though of course I was allowed to be here- it was a public library. One of the other grievers- I remembered his name at once, it was Mikey- was smiling benignly at me. I privately thought that Mikey was a bit strange. He smiled a lot, despite his deceased mother, and he dressed a bit like a hippie. Vests over shirts, that sort of thing. Maybe this was what provoked me to answer him.

"How do you know?"

I was alone much of the time now. I felt it like a great freezing landscape rippling outwards from me in a gush of ice; I felt the surrealism of my continued existence with the acuity of an explorer stranded on the tundra. This is what death does, I believe. It strands you.

"Bacteria," Mikey said, nonsensically. He wasn't wearing one of his vests tonight, just a flannel shirt in shades of grey and blue. I frowned.

"What, like germs?"

"Well, kind of." He took the other seat without such a by-your-leave. My sea ice creaked under his weight. "Did you know there are literally millions of bacteria living on your skin right now? Just hanging out. Doing their thing."

I realised I had gravely misjudged Mikey. Weird-but-harmless? Wrong assessment. If we'd been sat on a bench in a park, I'd have been edging away. Unfortunately, the library chairs weren't made for edging. They were one step away from beanbags; a gravitational black hole for the backside.

"Oh, no. You think that's gross, don't you?"

I admitted I did. Images of twitching petri dishes filled my head, multiplied a thousand times over and squirming over my body. Mikey shook his head with the enthusiasm of a wet dog.

"No, no! It's not gross! Literally how your body was designed. You've got entire communities depending on you for survival, for sustenance. In return, they look after you. It's kind of beautiful, actually."

I did the scales assessment so quickly it was almost subconscious: stay and listen to Mad Mikey, or go home and be physically, as well as functionally, alone. I subsided into the chair, the cushion emitting a mutual sigh.

"But bacteria give you infections," I said. "That's literally why we have antibiotics."

Mikey seemed immensely cheered by my willingness to engage. "Some bacteria give you infections. But there are millions and millions of species! Most of them don't hurt you. Some of them even help you." When I gave him a sceptical look, he nodded encouragingly. "Look it up!"

The scales assessment still, astonishingly, came out on the side of "stay and indulge him." I pulled out my phone and googled *bacteria on skin*. The NHS wanted to know if I had a staph infection. I guessed I probably didn't, but it sounded bad.

"This is only talking about infections," I said, a quiet note of triumph in my voice. Mikey did the wet dog head shake again.

"No, keep scrolling."

I did. *The Microorganisms That Live On Our Skin*. I opened it up. "Excuse me! Excuse me!"

Mikey and I poked our heads around the shelf like rabbits from a burrow. Heather, our chief coordinator, was speaking.

"I'm sorry to cut the party short, but the library's closing now. Thank you all for coming..."

I decided the universe was throwing me a lifeline. I visualised it, hauling myself out of the chair, hand over hand. "Bye, Mikey."

He unfolded himself with the ease of origami. "Bye, Sarah."

I sat on the sea ice later that night and ended up reading the article for something to do, somewhere else to be. I learned that most of the bacteria on my skin were, as Mikey said, *commensalistic* (did no harm) or *mutualistic* (leant a hand). Then I googled, *can bacteria survive in the arctic*, and it turned out they could. I wondered at that, looking down at the backs of my hands, imagining that petri dish again. With a swipe of my thumb, was I killing them? Was I more powerful than freezing, than an age of permafrost? The thought was strangely disturbing.

"I looked it up," I said to Mikey, when we next met after the support group. He looked genuinely delighted.

"Cool, isn't it! Wait 'til you look up the bacteria in your gut. That'll *really* blow your mind."

I wasn't expecting to laugh, but I did. It came out rusty and thickset. Not much cause for laughing on the tundra. "You're a strange one, Mikey," I told him. He took a bow.

He told me that he was a bacteria-vangelist, whatever that meant. He'd been studying for a biology degree before his mum was diagnosed; he'd dropped out to take care of her. He never seemed to want to linger on the tragedy of it. Instead, he loved his precious biology with a voracious, half-formed glee. He wanted nothing more than to share it with anyone who'd listen. I listened. It was surprisingly interesting.

"Sarah," he said, one night after the support group. "Do you think I smell?"

It was an off-the-cuff question. I balked with the practiced aversion of middle England; body odour? Not an acceptable topic of conversation. I made my best taken aback expression and watched the pigeons on the pavement (we were on the front steps; it was a tantalising spring evening; the railings were nice to lean against). Mikey didn't rush into the silence. He rarely did. It was something I'd grown to like about him.

"I only ask," he added, once a bus had wheezed past and he was sure I wasn't going to answer, "because I've stopped showering."

I blinked. Then a sly smile crept onto my face, sidling around the corner of my mouth.

"You know, they warn us about that sort of thing. Not showering. One of the key signs."

He laughed his easy laugh. A Mikey laugh, I'd started calling it, the kind that started in his shoulders and made them go loose like a puppet on a string. I eyed him in the wake of this revelation, but he didn't look like a cave creature. His brown hair was still tolerably clean; he wasn't smeared with dirt.

"I know, I know. But I promise it's not like that. I'm not depressed. I'm trying to look after my microbiome."

I rolled my eyes, but it was in a good-natured way. "You and your microbiome."

"*You* and your microbiome. We've all got one."

"Mm."

"Anyway. I'm pretty sure I don't smell, I mean, nobody at work is yelling," he mimed an expression of horror and flailed his hands, "and telling me to get away. But still. Thought I'd check."

"You don't smell," I said. When he raised his eyebrows, I shrugged my shoulder. "You don't!"

"Alright. Good."

We watched the pigeons for a while. The librarian was locking the door. The air smelled of the changing season and busy road.

"I got you something."

I turned my head. "Oh?"

He pulled a paper bag out of his pocket. "Soap."

I snorted. "After all that worrying about whether *you* smell."

"I didn't mean it like that! It's just this stuff is a bit more gentle. Plus-" he rustled the paper bag in an enticing manner, "- it's plastic free. Better, right?"

I accepted the gift. The bag smelled like a garden- in a nice way. "Thanks."

"And," he said, earnest now, "when I say not showering, I'm still *clean*. I still wash my hands and rinse my hair. I still use deodorant. Just not spray on stuff."

"Mikey. I've been using that stick stuff you were talking about for two months. I'm not judging you."

"Oh. Good."

The ice was melting on that hazy April evening. I felt it creak again. An instinctive fear of drowning clutched at my heart.

"It was a year ago on Tuesday," I found myself saying, addressing the words to a crack in the pavement. Mikey, as always, accepted this segue. He rearranged himself against the railing.

"Your dad?"

"Yeah."

Tight, dry throat. Not so bad. Not good, either.

"Anniversaries suck."

"Yeah."

I was crumpling the paper bag in between my fingers, giving myself a nose full of garden. More traffic. More Mikey silence.

"You know," I said, after a while, "I wasn't, well, doing good. For a while. After it happened. I kind of- wanted to give up. I really wanted to give up."

Mikey nodded. He understood. I stood up on the ice, watching the unknowable, unseen ocean all around me, feeling my floe rock in the waves.

"You're a good egg, Mikey."

He smiled, gentler than I expected. "You, too."

"Is it weird," I asked him, "to keep living for the non-sentient completely indifferent oblivious organisms existing on and in me right now?"

"No. Not weird."

I nodded. I hadn't planned it, really, but there was rosemary in my nose and hope in the air, and my dad had always wanted me to get out more.

"Mikey, fancy going to the pub?"

His face lit up. "I thought you'd never ask."

We walked down the road, not quite holding hands. The water was cold, but I was swimming, drawing eager breaths. When we stopped at the pedestrian crossing, Mikey cleared his throat.

"Did you know, they found a species of bacteria that only grows on the wall of one pub in England? It's where all the men would go outside to urinate. Their collective efforts resulted in a new species."

I bit down on a laugh. "You've been waiting to tell me that one."

He wrinkled his nose, Mikey laugh incoming. The sun fell on us as though straight from heaven, the last glorious rays of the day. The car engines could have been a serenade.

"Maybe," he said. "Maybe."

An Up and Coming Business

by Alyson Hilbourne

"Hello? How's my favourite used car salesman?"

I froze as a glacial shiver went down my spine and a brain freeze pain spread across my forehead. That was a voice I hadn't heard in a long time.

I was working late on a truck as a favour to a friend when footsteps crunched over the forecourt and stopped just in front of me. I slid the car creeper out from under the front of the truck and saw polished leather shoes, then crisp creased trousers and a tailored coat and finally I looked up into the granite-hewn face of Big Jim Stover.

I was immediately transported back to my school days.

"Cross me again, and I'll feed you to the worms!"

Big Jim had me pinned up against the coat pegs in the foyer, my feet scrabbling to touch the ground as his meaty fist held my collar and his face was inches from mine as he spat the words at me.

He was after my lunch money.

Again.

It didn't do to annoy Jim. His henchmen, buck-toothed Bob and freckly Phil, were standing by to finish me off if he gave the word. Jim issued the threats but he never got his hands dirty. Silently I handed over my coins.

It was no surprise I left school as soon as I could with few qualifications and a healthy respect for the rule of size.

I apprenticed in Dad's garage. The run-down wooden sheds and rusty petrol pumps stood on the edge of town. Unfortunately, the business was going nowhere as cars became computerised and people took their vehicles to specialist centres. We worked on puncture repairs and oil changes. Gradually Dad had to let staff go and when he retired, the garage, for what it was worth, came to me.

Big Jim went to work with his Dad as a bookie at the racecourse but he had ambition and soon progressed to running betting shops, first one in the Parade, then a chain of them across town. He swapped his warm anorak and flat cap for sharp suits and Armani jackets with cashmere roll neck sweaters. He smelled of aftershave, had his hands manicured and drove a Jaguar that he replaced each year. Wherever he went Bob and Phil shadowed him.

If I met Big Jim, and I tried not to, he'd ruffle my hair and ask how his favourite used car salesman was. The fact Dad and I had never sold cars, except perhaps as a favour to a friend, didn't bother him. The truth would have spoiled his joke and denied him the chance to sneer. We moved in different circles, but he had fingers in everything. A hotel was refurbished with his investment. He sponsored the kiddie's playground, financed a new housing estate and owned a nursery, a wedding venue and an undertaker's.

I wished I could move away but there was no chance of selling the garage for anything like what it had once been worth. The land was useless – a concrete and tarmac plot, with broken down sheds, piles of old tyres and drums of used oil. The scrubby paddock behind wouldn't support one sheep, let alone a flock and since the bypass had been built hardly anyone passed by anymore.

"I have a business proposition for you," Jim continued, looking down at me, still on the creeper. I wanted to slide back under the truck. "It's come to my attention that this place isn't doing too good." He pulled a mock sad face as he looked around. "You could do with a little investment."

I wanted nothing to do with him, but lying at his feet, so to speak, I was in no position to argue. I'd heard he was running drugs, protection, and extortion rackets. Rumour was that people who argued with him disappeared.

"It'll be worth your while. There's not much money in used cars."

A smirk flickered across Bob's face and it crossed my mind Jim only kept Bob and Phil on to laugh at his jokes, but they turned to the boot of Jim's car and hauled out a large bundle, wrapped in tarpaulin.

Phil grunted as they staggered across to me with it and Bob looked relieved when they dropped it unceremoniously on the ground.

"You have space," Jim said. "I need something buried." He looked towards the paddock. "Forever."

My dinner rose in my throat. It was obvious what the bundle contained. I didn't want to do Jim's dirty work.

Fleetingly I thought about going to the police, but one look at Jim's face reminded me that my life wouldn't be worth living. He bent towards me and I shrank back against the creeper, the plastic digging into my shoulder blades as I tried to stop myself shaking.

"For your trouble." He tucked a bundle of notes into the top pocket of my overalls, stood up, dusted off his hands and walked away.

When I'd stopped hyperventilating, I got to my feet. I hated myself for being weak but nobody argued with Jim.

I spent the next few hours digging a deep hole in the paddock. With an industrial mask over my face, I removed the tarpaulin and rolled the body into the hole and backfilled. In the morning, I scattered wildflower seeds, hoping to disguise the newly turned soil.

Over the winter Jim brought me two more bundles to dispose of. By the time summer arrived the paddock was a splendid meadow of flowers. Each time I caught a glimpse of it, it gave me a warm feeling inside, until I remembered why the flowers had grown so well.

This gave me an idea.

The land could become a graveyard. I could re-wild it and get rid of all traces of the garage business. I did my research. I looked up English wildflower meadows and sort out the best seeds to get. I found out how these would attract insects, birds and small mammals. I got various local wildlife groups on board with the idea and enlisted their help.

I applied to the council. I proposed "a green graveyard" with burial in coffins made of recycled cardboard. The coffins would be topped up with soil and a mix of wildflower seeds chosen by the mourners. It would be cheaper than a regular funeral and would create a vibrant meadow.

Win win.

The council took some persuading.

"We don't want bodies buried all over our area," one councillor said.

I persuaded them the plots would be carefully contained.

No spillage.

"Growing plants helps sequester carbon," I told them. "And the bodies add nutrients to plants. They grow better and stronger and store more carbon. They may also help remove some of the heavy metals from the atmosphere that increasing road usage is producing.

The breakdown of the organic matter will increase the overall microbial population of the soil too, and the microbes perform powerful functions such as nutrient cycling, stimulating plant growth, nitrogen-fixing, suppression of pests and improving soil health." I could see at least one councillor going cross-eyed trying to get his head around the ideas. He obviously finished school with the same qualifications I did...

But eventually the council were persuaded. They were keen to increase their green credentials and meet government carbon neutral requirements and the last thing they wanted to do was introduce a green air zone and charge road users to come into the town as they knew that would provoke an outcry. They were happy to try anything.

I was granted a licence. I encouraged mourners to choose native seeds like red clover, ox-eye daisies, and harebells. Poppies and wild orchids were popular, and buttercups and cornflowers grew without seeding. I tore down the sheds, cleared the oil and tyres, chipped up the concrete and converted the whole of the garage site to the graveyard.

The first burial was a sad affair. I'd laid a central path through the plot but the rest of it was bare earth. I saw the deceased relatives looking round dubiously.

"It's horrible," I heard one say. "Couldn't we have gone for a cremation?"

The man's daughter was tough though.

"This will be beautiful in a couple of years. Just give it time to grow. Nothing happens overnight."

She was right. After a couple of years the change to the land was significant and we had became a popular attraction in the town, with the school bringing children to identify plants and butterflies and families coming to remember the dead and enjoy the wilderness on the edge of the urban area. Burial plots weren't marked as such but I did maintain a map so if people wanted to know where their relatives were buried I could tell them roughly. Mostly however, those that came to visit were happy to enjoy the meadow, the quiet and the beauty of the place.

The green graveyard was firmly on the map. Other towns asked for advice and I started green graveyards all round the country. Some places wanted native woodlands rather than meadows, so I sourced a nursery to help with native young trees. Business was blooming.

"How is my favourite used car salesman?"

I jumped. Big Jim, drink in hand, had crept up on me at a town event held to raise more awareness of climate change and global warming.

"Fine, thank you."

I looked for a way to escape but Jim had positioned himself in front of me, while Phil and Bob, out of place in dinner jackets and half strangled by their bow ties, were a little way behind.

"You know you're taking business away from me?" Jim purred.

I swallowed.

"A drop of thirty percent in funerals at Graves and Partners this year. It's not right," Jim said. "We have an aging population. Funerals should be a safe bet but it seems like people are choosing this green option you're offering. I don't like it. I don't like it one bit."

He pointed a finger at me — a finger that got dangerously close to stabbing me in the chest.

His message was clear.

I left the event. As I went down the steps outside, a hand grabbed my collar and I was dragged into the shadows.

"You heard the boss?" Freckly Phil yanked my arm up behind my back making me whimper and stand on tiptoe to relieve the pain. He wrenched my arm up to emphasise what he was saying.

"Business isn't as good." Wrench.

"As it." Wrench.

"Should be." Wrench.

I gasped.

He let go of me and I fell forward.

"Sort it or we'll feed you to the worms."

Buck-toothed Bill growled his agreement and they turned and climbed up the steps.

I returned to the graveyard, nursing my shoulder and trying to calm my breathing. I sat on a bench and listened to the night insects. Occasionally I caught sight of a bat in the moonlight. I didn't want to be intimidated, but you didn't argue with Big Jim, not if you didn't want to push up the daisies yourself.

I had a problem.

Meanwhile, I heard on the grapevine that local gangs were moving in and Jim was struggling to maintain his hold on his gambling empire. Fights involving gang members and raids on each other's premises were becoming a regular occurrence across town.

Still, I had almost decided to declare the graveyard full and stop burials, when an argument at a nightclub turned nasty and there was a shooting. The victim was Big Jim.

His wife came to see me.

"I want a green funeral for my Jim," she said.

It was the least I could do.

On the day, his wife, dressed in black with a veil over her face, was supported by her two children. I'd heard neither was interested in taking over the family business.

Buck-toothed Bob and freckly Phil, in dark suits and dark glasses, stood back. They looked around constantly, worried no doubt by the possibility of more reprisals.

I told the mourners how Jim's burial would encourage grasshoppers, butterflies, moths, bees, and small birds. Within a year a beautiful show of flowers would appear from the spot where he was buried.

Jim would have hated it.

I heard his widow sob as the coffin was lowered into the ground. One last look and the family turned to go, leaving me with the buzzing insects and the smell of turned soil.

Alone, I leaned down until my face was inches from Jim's cardboard tomb.

"Enjoy the worms, Jim," I said. "And thanks for the business."

I stood up, dusted my hands, and walked away.

Up Shit's Creek

by Brian Adams

"**A**re you there?" Anna shouted, cradling her phone on her shoulder. "Can you hear me?"

Anna balanced precariously on the top rung of a stepladder, stretching to plug the last extension cord into the highest outlet. She pumped her fist in the air as the water pump once again roared back to life. Hopping off the ladder, she raced back outside.

"I'm knee-deep in shit here, Bart! Do you understand?"

"Of course I do." Bart's voice was slurred, either from sleep or drink. Probably the latter, Anna thought.

"I mean literally knee deep. It's practically flowing over my boots! One more foot and we're totally screwed. You need to get your sorry ass down here, now!"

This was clearly not the way to talk to your boss, but with the rain coming down and the river still rising, Anna was desperate.

She heard a glass clink as another sip was taken.

"How about Ted?" Bart asked, the slur even stronger. "And Rusty? Have you- "

"They're already here, damn it. You were on call tonight, Bart. You're supposed to be the one in charge! It's all hands-on deck and, goddammit, you're AWOL! Again!"

"Now, now. Let's not go overboard." The glass clinked again.

"Son-of-a-bitch!" Anna whispered, not quite loud enough for the son-of-a-bitch to hear.

She hung up and stashed her phone in her coveralls. This man, her *boss*, was the head of the sewage treatment plant. Here they were, up shit's creek and barely keeping afloat, and *this* was how he acted?

~~~

Anna had been mid-bite into a yummy stuffed mushroom hors d'oeuvres at her favorite vegetarian restaurant when she got the text. It was her third date with Scarlett, the gorgeous redhead she was desperately trying to impress. Scarlett was a buyer for a high-end clothing store and the challenge was this: she was a sartorial femme who wore pink and pastel tailored pants and jumpsuits. While she didn't look like Barbie, she sure dressed like her. Anna dressed up nice, but Scarlett? Wow! That woman was in a different league.

Plus, Scarlett always smelled of Delina Exclusif Eau de Parfum, while Anna, after a long shift at work, was constantly paranoid about smelling like Eau de Crap. She had explained how she worked in a "public health facility" which, though true, was a bit of a stretch. But damn if she wasn't struggling with the "I work with poop" reveal.

Anna stuffed a final bite of mushroom into her mouth. She usually kept her phone stashed safely away during dates, but while Scarlett was in the bathroom, she had noticed a glow from her bag under the table and couldn't help but check the text.

"I am so sorry," Anna said, "but I have to bounce."

"Oh no!" Scarlett reached out and put her hand on Anna's. "Is everything okay?" Anna caught her breath. That first touch was electrifying.

"Work," she said. "This damn rain. We're getting flooded out!"

"Your office?" Scarlett looked confused.

"Not really my office. The sewage treatment plant. That's where I work. The Green River has overflowed and the - "

"Shit has hit the fan?"

Anna smiled at the quick retort. "Let's hope not. Fingers crossed!"

Scarlett reached out and criss-crossed her fingers with Anna's. "Is there anything I can do?" Scarlett asked.

"Get out that pink umbrella of yours and do a rain dance. One that zips up the clouds." "Got it. Text me later? To let me know you're okay?"

"Will do." Anna took a deep breath and hurried out of the restaurant.

~~~

Ever since she was a little girl, Anna was fascinated with bugs. The smaller the better. While other kids might back away in alarm, Anna would squeal with delight at the sight of a squash beetle or a daddy longlegs. Her favorite nursery rhyme was the Eensy Weensy Spider, and she drove her parents half-crazy demanding they recite it over and over.

"How small is eensy weensy?" Anna would ask her mum. "Pretty darn small," mum would answer.

"Smaller than this?" Anna would hold her chubby little fingers as close together as she could.

"Maybe even smaller, darling."

In seventh grade, Anna had a science teacher who changed her life. Introduced to microscopes for the first time, she adjusted the eyepiece and was gobsmacked to view microorganisms that made eensy weensy look titanic. Until then, she had thought living things were either plants or animals, but now the whole world of microscopic life came stunningly into focus. Single-celled organisms, like bacteria, reproducing by splitting in two. Shape shifting amoeba extending and retracting prehistoric armlike structures. Predatory protozoans engulfing other single-celled creatures.

Science became her thing, and as she excelled in AP high school biology and chemistry it was clear she had a calling. Accepted into the honors program in microbiology at the University of Massachusetts, she was a teaching assistant by the time she was a junior, undertaking graduate level research in microbial bioremediation as a senior.

Bioremediation – using microbes to remove environmental contaminants. She was so excited - *turned on* even - by the idea that, for her thesis presentation, she accidentally titled her PowerPoint presentation *Orgasms At Work For You* rather than *Organisms*. She received the highest of marks from all of her professors.

Never one to back away from what others found disgusting, the field of sewage treatment was an endless source of fascination for her. Pools full of oxygen demanding waste (i.e., shit) were chomped on by millions, no, billions of microorganisms. What was not to love about that? After all, one woman's waste was another creature's dinner.

While she was still in college, her stepsister had married a man from India and the wedding was held in Bangalore, India's third largest city. She was a bridesmaid and, in between frantically arranging flowers and ordering food, she managed to slip away and visit one of the sewage treatment plants. Not your usual tourist destination. The plant wasn't nearly up to task to handle the many millions who lived there, particularly during the torrential monsoon rains when most sewage flowed untreated into the Vrishabhavat River.

The visit had a profound effect on her. Diseases and contagions from untreated sewage ran rampant, and the devastation to India's waterways, as vibrant rivers turned into ecological disaster zones, was heartbreaking.

Her senior year she landed an internship as a biochemist at the town's water quality lab. Following graduation, she was offered a full-time job. One opportunity led to another and now, with her certification completed as a wastewater technician I and II, she was practically running the place.

~~~

Anna gritted her teeth and charged outside. Rusty, Ted and two part-timers from the Department of Public Works were piling sand-bags around the four secondary treatment pools, the last-gasp effort to keep the still rising Green River out.

"Build the wall!" Anna shouted. "Build the wall!" Damn! Those were Trumpian words she never dreamed she'd hear come out of her mouth. Her friends would disown her for yelling that kind of shit.

She sprinted to the bucket loader to fill it with another round of sandbags. *If the good Lord was willing and the creek don't rise.* That was how the old time saying went. But that was before climate change, right? Now the good Lord seemed pretty pissed, and all bets were off.

It seemed to Anna as if it never rained normal anymore, it only rained crazy. This was the third 'once in a hundred years' rain event since the fourth of July, and it was stunning what three inches in three hours could do to the usually placid Green River. With seepage from saturated soils sneaking their way into aging underground sewage pipes, the plant was just barely handling the inflow. And now, even with the rain tapering off, the overflowing river was still marching forward.

If they couldn't keep the floodwaters out of the secondary treat-ment pools, untreated contaminated sewage would be released down-stream. And her bugs! Her precious microorganisms that did so much of the work for her! If the secondary pools were breached, those critters would be swept away.

Teensy, weensy as they were, those microbes were the heavy hitters of the sewage treatment plant. It wasn't her, Ted or Rusty, it wasn't those two guys from the DPW whose names she could never remember, it certainly wasn't her slacker of a boss who should have retired a decade ago. It was the Betaproteobacteria with their voracious appetite for shit. Anna fondly referred to them as the Beta Brunch Bunch, the ones who munched on yesterday's lunch. There were other organisms with equally cool sounding names – stalked ciliates, rotifers, and, her favorite, tardigrades, also called water bears. Their motto was eat shit and die. She loved every single one of them.

"Build the wall!" Anna screamed through the rain, dumping yet another bucket loader full of sandbags at the edge of the pool.

~~~

Anna's phone vibrated. She stopped momentarily to check the message. It wasn't Bert calling in reinforcements, but something almost as good.

Just making sure you're okay, Scarlett's text read. And then, even better: *Thinking about you*.

~~~

One of the favorite parts of Anna's job was giving tours to school groups. She loved the looks on kids' faces when they saw the toilet in her office filled with geraniums, the notice on the bathroom door that read "donation center," and the sign prominently displayed on her desk: *THE SHIT STOPS HERE*.

For all its high-tech complexities, sewage treatment wasn't that difficult to understand.

Sewage from almost every residence and business in town traveled through an intricately connected series of small diameter underground pipes that fed into larger and larger pipes, ultimately spilling into one pipe that fed the plant.

In primary treatment, solids settled to the bottom of tanks larger than swimming pools.

The solids were removed as sludge, and the liquids traveled on to secondary treatment. "It's as simple as that," Anna would explain. "Solid stuff sinks, light stuff floats."

"Eww" kids would squeal, holding their noses, as Anna scooped up a net full of sludge.

Anna got it. On a warmish day, it was like opening the door to an overused outhouse.

"Awesome," other kids would yell with even greater gusto, undeterred by olfactory overload.

Secondary treatment was where the real magic happened. That's where Anna's bugs did their thing. Those treatment tanks were like heaven to them. The rich array of wonderfully diverse microorganisms ate shit to their hearts' content and then died. Actually, they didn't really have hearts, or brains for that matter, but if they had, they would have leapt out of the water and given a big thumbs up to Anna.

"Thanks for everything!" they would have yelled. "It was delicious!"

Soon their lifeless, bloated bodies would sink to the bottom of the secondary treatment settling tanks and be removed as sludge.

Oxygen demanding waste, left untreated, could enter the river and cause naturally occurring bacteria's numbers to skyrocket. This would deplete oxygen levels in the water so necessary for fish and other organisms. No oxygen meant no aquatic life.

"Organisms at work for you!" Anna would shout out to students over the din of the giant bubblers as they pumped oxygen into the tanks.

"Awesome!" kids would yell. "Eww!" shouted others.

The last stop of the tour was where the effluent was chlorinated to kill what pathogens remained, dechlorinated, and then pumped into the Green River pretty darn clean. Kids were impressed.

~~~

What if Anna was to bring Scarlett on a tour? What would Scarlett think? *Eww* or *Awesome*?

Focus! Anna told herself, wiping the rain out of her eyes and loading up the bucket with another round of sandbags. Her love life had to wait. The task at hand was keeping the river from flooding the tanks.

Thank goodness she had forced Bart to teach her how to use the bucket loader. And how to reposition pumps in case of emergencies like this? And where to position sandbags to re-route flood waters. Those, and a ton of other essentials, were nowhere to be found in her job description or her pay grade but, dammit, someone had to know how to right the ship when the captain was nowhere to be found.

Ted, Rusty, and the two whatever-their-names-were were looking to her expectantly for direction. She wasn't their boss but, with Bart increasingly shirking his duties, she was the one calling the shots. This was the third time this month they'd faced a do-or-die crisis like this. The third friggin time! With climate change rearing its ugly head, emergencies like these were the new normal.

"The bastard has got to be retiring soon!" her roommate Clara had argued when Anna had come home once again bitching about her boss. "You should take the job. The first woman sewage treatment plant director in the state! Wouldn't that be a hoot!"

Maybe Clara was right. Bart's days were numbered. If she had anything to do with it, he'd have retired yesterday. And then, maybe, she should apply for his position. Would that garner awe from a woman like Scarlett? But. if Anna was to be the director of the treatment plant, then there had to be a plant to direct, and, with the water still rising ...

~~~

"To the left!" Anna ordered. "Stack up the rest of the bags. Three high. We've got to channel the flow toward the slope where the river willows are!!"

Anna and Rusty dragged another pump over to where pooling water was lapping at the secondary tank. Another few inches rise and she could kiss her bugs goodbye. Swept away was not okay.

If they could just divert the flow a little to the left. She rushed back to the bucket loader for the final round of sandbags. The rain had stopped but the river was still angry. A few more sandbags, A repositioning of the pump hose. Just a little more to the left ...

~~~

"Wow!" Scarlett said. "Sounds like some evening!"

Anna had texted her smiling, dancing emojis when she had finally gotten home, exhausted, at three that morning. The crisis had been averted. The wall of sandbags had held. The pumps had kept the flood at bay. Her precious bugs had survived to do their thing, at least until the next high water.

"You're like a hero!" Scarlett gushed.

Anna laughed. "Thanks, but let's not push it."

It was Friday night, two days after the flood waters had receded. They were back at the same restaurant, the same table in fact, and Anna was happily feasting on the stuffed mushroom hors d'oeuvres, hoping to finish them uninterrupted this time.

"I'm dating a celebrity!" Scarlett held up the day's local newspaper. There was a picture of Anna standing next to the treatment pool, a bemused look on her face. "*Savior of the Sewage* it reads. Front page, no less."

"Of the B section," Anna replied, blushing.

"And it says the Director, Bart something-or-other, is going to retire. Does that mean you're taking over?"

Anna shook her head. "Too soon for that. I haven't even decided whether to apply or not."

"What?" Scarlett reached over and helped herself to a forkful of Anna's mushrooms.

"You definitely should. You know why?" "Why?" Anna answered.

Scarlett reached over and took Anna's hand in hers. "Because you'll be . . . awesome!"

For the Common Good

by Prashant Vaze

My attention has been focused on Hamish Macrae since ten this morning. The lid of the fountain pen in his top pocket is fitted with a minuscule camera. Hamish's shift is due to end soon. On the CCTV I watch him perform a last check on the microbial cultures, dim the light so they can multiply in peace, lean over the wastepaper basket, log off his console, retrieve his car keys from his closet, and make for the door.

Time for our rendezvous.

My hobby, as a kid, was cracking security puzzles; others saw it as hacking. My parents were terrified I would end up in prison. Instead, I got a job at GCHQ. Worse of both worlds, crap money, crap working conditions. After thirty years, they gave me my gold watch.

I wear my poker face as Hamish (no longer wearing the fountain pen) tries to pass me in the corridor. He doesn't acknowledge me. Why should he? Two hundred people work each shift at the facility.

I thrust my arm out, catching him on his head. I am six-six. At school, the lads used to call me Jack Reacher. The original badass Lee Child version, not the Tom Cruise.

It's fascinating watching his anger rise to a boil, simmer, and turn to bafflement. All in three seconds. He squints trying to recall who I am. "You're that guy from HR, aren't you? The one who checks the security questionnaires."

"Milo Fletcher. Head of security." I grip his wrist tight and yank it behind his back, so he understands there is no such thing as free will, not under the terms and conditions he signed up to. "You and me, we need to see Rhys." I march him back to the room he just exited, where I grab his paper bin. Together, we go to the Rhys' office. I knock and enter. "Mr Rhys. Here's the lad we talked about earlier, Hamish Macrae."

Rhys Logan looks like a bald red hamster, with a ginger beard. I put on some plastic gloves and take the wastepaper bin over to Rhys. He watches as I fish out the pen. "What have we here?"

"It's just a pen," Hamish splutters. "Someone must have thrown it away."

I take out my tablet and show his image from this morning wearing a pen in his breast pocket.

"Careless of you to lose it like that. It's rather fancy."

Macrae shrugs. "The two pens look completely different. The one on your laptop has a bead on the tip."

I am perturbed to see that the bead, which I assume contains the memory fleck, is missing from the pen I just retrieved. I maintain my poker face and open up the pen's barrel. There's a small cage with a bijoux circuit and a cornea of glass.

"A tiny camera! You didn't pick this up off eBay. Macrae, you've been spying on us. We need to ask you some questions."

We can't interrogate him here. Rhys works in a goldfish bowl. Both the office's internal walls are glass. On the other side, boffins in plastic hairnets and gowns are monitoring the kelp and bacteria communities in huge drums.

I say to Rhys. "Do you mind you taking him to the conference room? I need to do something urgent." I go to my team at the reception and order them to cancel this evening's waste collection and make sure everyone goes through the metal detector on the way out. "Shoes and belts off – the full works. No personal electronics that have been inside the premises can leave."

When I get to the conference room, Rhys is emptying out its previous occupants. "Och! Joseph, the lads look knackered. Let them go home to pretend they'd rather be putting their wee ones to bed than still here saving the world."

I glance around. There's a Gaia BioFuels corporate plaque with the company's bullshit mission *For the Common Good* next to a framed photo of our CEO Xander Deshpande shaking hands with the then-PM Rishi Sunak. A pre-beard, still-hirsute Rhys lurks in the background of the photo. I forget he worked his way up through the ranks. Fifteen years ago, when Gaia BioFuels first started, he skippered the boat that seeded the firm's first-ever Scottish kelp farm. A dial on the wall reads 155,345,206 tCO_2. That's how much carbon the company's kelp forests have sequestered since then.

I stare at the whiteboard with the departed scientists' work. It shows electron telescope images of fronds covered with brightly coloured stumpy rods and dots. The researchers here are mainly marine ecologists who prospect for new strains of bacteria to culture on the kelp. The scientists' contracts prohibit them from talking openly, but you can't help but pick up their love for their work. As a side gig, apart from sequestering carbon, the kelp hosts bacterial communities which remove ocean pollutants.

I hand Rhys the dossier I compiled on Hamish. He takes his time reading it. Hamish stares around the room.

I take in a deep breath of air savouring the sulphurous stink of kelp. Its bouquet permeates every room, every crevice, every piece of furniture. The local Uber drivers charge us to cleanse their cabs after a pickup.

"What's on that pen?" asks Rhys, voice as cold as a dip in Loch Ness.

"Not mine." Hamish looks away peeved.

His 'tell' is looking away when he lies. While he's auditioning for Hamlet, I spray the pen with a dye to reveal the fingerprints on the barrel and use my laptop's GPT to compare the fingerprints on the barrel with my file of staff fingerprints. The laptop confirms a match with Hamish's.

"It must have been in my jacket pocket. My girlfriend got it for me. As far as I know, it's just a normal pen."

I guffaw. "Who is your girlfriend? 'Q'?"

Hamish shrugs. "It's not a crime to accidentally bring a camera to the office. Have you got any evidence I stole any information?"

Rhys looks at me pointedly. I can see he wants something too. "What's your role at Gaia BioFuels?" I ask to change the topic. "I'm just a humble technician in the microbiology lab."

"Who did you assist today?"

Hamish pauses to think. "I ran some bacterial DNA through the gene sequencer, then sent the results to the scientist requesting the work. Disposed of some old petri dishes."

"Tell us exactly what rooms you went to today and how long you spent in each one."

Hamish cooperates.

Rhys traces around his lips with his tongue. "Milo put together some stills from the CCTV footage of you over the day. It shows you, and your camera pen, browsing through our *methods and standard operating procedures manual,* systematically scrolling through our database of bacterial genomes. I reckon you've video-ed the DNA sequence of half a dozen bacteria strains."

"Listen pal, I was doing my job. I enter data on the database and error check old records. But you make it sound like I was doing something criminal. He's lying about me." He gives Rhys a knowing grin which is wilted by Rhys's gaze.

Rhys passes the dossier to me.

"On your CV you neglected to mention you'd got a degree in microbiology from the Open University. On your LinkedIn profile, I see you've done a short course on data science. I'm used to seeing people making up fake qualifications, not people hiding them."

"No comment."

Rhys leans over, "Listen, *pal*, you know why we are here don't you?"

"To get me to confess? To set me up? You accuse me of stealing information. Where is it? All you've got is photos of me doing my job."

Rhys shakes his head sadly. "I don't get you. You've been part of our family for six months. You're working with some of the most talented microbiologists in the world. Our mission is to help the world recover from climate change and clean up the oceans. Still you betray us?" Rhys pushes a pad of paper over. "Who else in the company is helping you? Who is pulling the strings outside? Give us some names."

"No comment." We sit in silence for five minutes. Hamish resumes his staring around the room. Finally, he says, "Am I under arrest?"

"We aren't police," Rhys growls.

"I want to go home. You got nae evidence I've stolen anything."

You have to admire Rhys's persistence. "Who's helping you? Who are you working for? Give us this information, and you'll *just* be sacked. If you don't cooperate, we will press charges. You will spend time in prison, and the legal fees will bankrupt you."

"You've got nuthun'."

I glance at the clock. "Let's take a five-minute break. Not you." I push Hamish roughly back into his seat. Rhys and I exit the corridor to stretch our legs and take a comfort break.

After my daily ration of a cigarette, I return to the corridor. Rhys asks. "What do you think?"

"He's working alone. He knew which bacterial strains he was after. But I'm certain the data is still on the premises."

"Any clue who he's working for?"

"Your guess is as good as mine. Too amateur to be a foreign government. More likely a competitor, or even one of the protestors outside. People hate us from all walks of life."

"The stink of fermenting kelp doesn't enamour us to the locals either," grumbles Rhys.

"Should we let him stew for a wee while longer?"

Sadly, the interrogation techniques we used back in Kandahar aren't available in a corporate environment. I shake my head. "We have to let him go."

"How are ye gonna find out who he's working for? Beat the crap out of him."

"Sorry. You don't need to know. Plus, you're not my boss." That was ruder than I intended.

"It's a delicate moment for the company. Lots of moving parts."

Rhys stiffens. "As I'm aware. The IPO is just a month away, and even the suspicion of a data breach will hurt the company's valuation. I've two more suspects for yer list. Big Pharma will be interested in our techniques to enhance the entanglement between the kelp and the bacteria. Our guys have proved if a school of fish graze the kelp, bacteria up to fifty metres away will start producing toxins to repel the fish species. This entanglement, Jeez it's like a telepathic air defence system."

I smile politely pretending I care. "Right then, I'll escort Hamish off the premises."

"Aren't you forgetting something?" Rhys eyebrows my pocket. I hand over Hamish's pen with the spy camera.

I look at Rhys. "You really love this company, don't you?"

"I guess so. Xander and his wife are building something great here. If anyone can save the oceans, it's them." He frowns at me. "What about you, old man? You've got a fat civil service pension; why are you here?"

"You don't like me much, do you?" I feel sorry for Rhys. You should never fall in love with your work, it never loves you back.

"Nothing personal. I dunna like spooks. Your moral compass is missin'."

Rhys takes the spy pen and returns to his office. There's a camp bed tucked away and he often sleeps there.

I retrieve Hamish from the interview room and escort him to the main entrance, where I make him strip before I put him and his gear through the metal detector. He retrieves his phone in the external locker. As well as his fingerprints, we also have high-resolution images of his face and iris. I hacked the phone a few hours ago. His life is mine to peruse.

We step out. The September night sky is as red as a murder scene, and a gust rifles through the pines. In summer there would be half a dozen protestors outside. Religious nut jobs, workers from the oil and gas sector protesting against our carbon credit income, disgruntled fishermen angry the kelp fields have encroached on their fishing pit-stops and ignoring the fact the fishery is much healthier. Today there's just the one weirdo. Her placard reads: "God creates life, companies create strife – no copyrighting of DNA." I've never understood why all these data campaigner types think it's okay to have intellectual property protection for music and their crappy books, but that the Deshpande family should give away their know-how for free.

As Hamish walks past her, I notice a slight shake of the head. The woman's name is Fiona St Ives. She started her vigil around the same time Hamish started to work here. Worth checking her out again.

I go back in and make the desk guards put every binbag through the scanner, metals inspected before being taken out. I keep my eye on the outside CCTV and notice Fiona stroll around the back of the facility where the waste is usually piled outside for pickup. Sorry luv, not on my watch. I send the security guards home at eight and continue by myself. At ten past eight, just as I hoped, the scanner finds the data fleck in a petri dish in a blue hazardous waste bag.

I pocket the data fleck and take it home.

Now I need to figure out his buyer. I spend the night going on Hamish's phone going through social media (mainly on Celtic FC and Scottish punk music), checking out his cash flow (breaking even), feeling irritated by his politics (mildly libertine littered with cliches about freedom) and checking his Amazon purchases (modest but with a wish list wildly beyond his means). He enjoys flirting with girls from the Ceilidh and got lucky with one or two lasses. A few minutes before two in the morning, I whisper bingo. I've decoded the WhatsApp communications between Hamish and his handler.

Feeling self-congratulatory, I go outside and treat myself to another smoke. Shivering, I stare at the picture-perfect starry night and think about my departing conversation with Rhys. The 'no moral compass' jibe upsets me. The truth is I didn't get a gold watch after thirty years' service to His Majesty's Government, just a weekend break at the local spa. Also, the civil service pension isn't what it used to be.

I have the data, and I know Hamish's handler. What's to stop me from selling her the data? We live in a free market economy. She'd gone to the trouble of installing Hamish in the company for six months. A million would be enough to buy me somewhere nice, away from the stink of kelp.

There's a missed call on my phone. Xander Deshpande. I straighten my T-shirt and comb my hair.

Mr Deshpande picks up straight away. Behind him, I see the hot sun blushing from behind clouds and a film poster in Indian script. He must be at the new algae processing facility in Navi Mumbai. He wears his hair in a long ponytail and has the musculature of someone who spends more on personal trainers than on champagne and fine wines.

"What you got?" His eyes are alert and inquisitive. Straight to the point, I like that about him.

"He was working alone. None of our data has been compromised."

"So, need to trouble Suzy." He stays on the line like he's waiting for something. "Any leads on who was the buyer?"

I shake my head. "The buyer was interested in the data itself, not in disrupting the IPO. The spy could have napalmed the facility's IT; instead, he went on a shopping trip. Procedural manuals, recent bacterial genomes from the database, photos and schema of the equipment."

"Which genomes?"

I read out the dates the DNA was sequenced. "Your wife will know what the boffins worked on back then."

Mr Deshpande looks thoughtful. "As it happens, so do I. Six months ago, we found a strain that eats microplastics. We were going to announce it a week before the IPO." He cups his hands into a yin and yang shape. "You know bacteria and kelp's relationship is complicated. Hundreds of different bacteria species live on the kelp. The bacteria fight off infection and liberate nutrients like sulphur and nitrogen; in return they receive sugars. Sometimes the bacteria turn on the kelp. They know its vulnerabilities and will kill it and take what they need. They cooperate but have a gun to one another's temples. This mutually assured destruction allowed them to thrive together in the cold Atlantic for 15 million years. Survival of the fittest implies an all-out war. It's not true."

"Sorry, Mr Deshpande, I don't understand your meaning."

"We were going to make information about the microplastic clearing community freely available a week before the IPO. Give something back to the world. Someone wanted to derail us. Can you find out who and pay them a call? I want their affiliations and intentions. If they wanted to profit or hurt us, if the first we go Darwinian on their balance sheet. But if their motives are less selfish...then I want to meet them."

After the call, I crawl into bed and sleeplessly stare at the ceiling. At six wearing my duvet, I step out for some fresh air and light my third cigarette in 24 hours. I think of the communities of bacteria and how they sometimes support the kelp and sometimes victimise it.

What was Deshpande saying to me? Did he know I had already worked out Rhys's buyer?

Xander Deshpande and his wife move in mysterious ways.

I imagine the hundreds of people tirelessly working at Gaia Biofuels, spending all night in their offices, neglecting their children and their spouses. All for the company's mission: For the common good.

I will arrange a meeting with Hamish's handler as Mr Deshpande asks. But what will I say when I meet her? Will I sell her the contents, or will I do as my boss asks?

Interview with a Microbe

by Helen Anderson

E lla: Hello listeners, and welcome to the Ella Salmon weekly Science podcast. The only podcast you need, for all things relating to science.

This week I am chatting with Mike Robe. For those of you who don't know, Mike is a top-level employee at the Three Oaks wastewater treatment plant in Lincoln. Mike achieved his Doctorate in Biotechnology from the prestigious Micro University in Miniscule.

Good morning, Mike and welcome to the studio.

Mike: Thanks for inviting me, Ella. It's an honour to be here. I am a *huge* fan of your podcasts. Excuse the pun. (Laughing). I always listen in to keep up to date with new scientific discoveries.

Ella: Firstly, let me say that when I completed my degree in journalism, I never expected that one day I would interview a single-celled microorganism. Especially one who spends his days dealing with digesting everyone else's poo. So, tell us Mike, what exactly *is* your role at Three Oaks and how *do* you spend your days at work?

Mike: (laughing) Well Ella, I don't get my hands dirty these days. I don't even have any hands (chuckles). As you may be aware, I was recently appointed as the CEM (Chief Executive Microbe) for Three Oaks which is a waste stabilisation pond facility. In this role I oversee all the daily operations and ensure that the employees are doing their assigned jobs correctly. If anyone slackens off, I'm right there to get them moving again. As you can imagine, this doesn't win me too many friends.

Ella: I can understand that. No-one likes slow-moving poo. Most people, including me, wouldn't even know how a wastewater treatment plant works. We just take the entire process for granted when we flush the toilet or have a shower. We naively assume the water just magically disappears down the drain and that's all there is to it. No one even gives it a second thought. So, in layman's terms, could you explain to our listeners how the wastewater treatment plant works?

Mike: No problem, Ella. So, to put it in very simple terms, when the wastewater comes in from the sewer system, it is screened to remove solid items, rubbish, and sediments. You'd be amazed to see what makes it into the sewerage systems. Basically, anything that will fit through the sewer pipes could end up in there. From dirty nappies to car parts, and everything in between.

The next step is for our teams of bacteria and protozoa to work in harmony, to produce the delicious, sweet-smelling sludge that can be seen floating on top of the settling ponds. Air is then pumped through the liquid, introducing oxygen into the mix. This process looks much like a fountain spouting in the ponds. It's like being in a spa. I love being in the ponds when aeration is happening. It's very relaxing.

The microbes and other bacteria in the liquid need this oxygen to help them digest the impurities. A couple of partially decomposed rat corpses thrown in for good measure also increases the taste (laughs). Just kidding. Mmmmm. I can almost smell it now.

Teamwork is crucial to the process. If the bacteria team, headed by Anna Robic, took a day off for the annual Decomp Picnic, it could cause problems for the protozoa team. Likewise, if the protozoa team leader, Ohmee Barr, decided to take her workers off on a team building activity, the bacteria team would struggle. One team on its own would not be efficient. We need all available staff to be present every day to ensure the plant works at maximum efficiency.

Ella: So how many staff are on site at Three Oaks on any given day?

Mike: More than a million staff members can be hard at work in each millilitre of wastewater. Can you imagine how hard it is to find a parking spot on site? On top of this, everyone needs to arrive at work early because the line-up to clock on is phenomenal. Oh, and don't get me started about the line-up to clock *off* at the end of shift. Let me put it this way, if you don't believe the dead come back to life, you should be here at knock-off time. (Laughing).

Our team members work around the clock, 24/7. The process never stops. When staff have their lunch break, others eagerly come forward to take their place. If staff were to go on strike, well let me say, the whole place would go to shit. Oops, can I say that on air?

Ella: That's okay Mike, we bleeped it out in time. (Laughs). Well, that certainly does sound daunting. So, tell me, on an average day, how much wastewater can be treated at your facility? And what happens to the wastewater after treatment?

Mike: Our treatment plant can cycle through 5-6 Megalitres every day. After the water is treated, several million of the workers will accompany the recycled water when it is sent off for irrigation of golf courses and playing fields. Millions more microbes are detained in the sludge ponds. These are the nastier ones. We can't afford to have rogue microbes running rampant out there in the community. We also utilise some of the recycled water for washing down surfaces and equipment on site.

Ella: What did you do before coming to work at Three Oaks?

Mike: Before I came to work here, I had a successful role working on a decomposing carcass. This is where I gained a fair amount of my organisational and management skills. Decomposition is a complex process; you can't just go in there and begin munching. It must be conducted in a certain manner. Unfortunately, that job site continually got smaller, until eventually there was no work for any of us and the site was shut down. I really miss the smell of that place though. The aroma of raw sewage just doesn't compare. And the flies, I miss them too. I had so many six-legged friends back there in Carcasstown. Louie was the best mate a microbe could ask for. He was always there beside me, helping us to spread the joy. Sometimes, I would even hitch a ride on his legs and he would transport me to other nearby decomp sites for a night out. It was a very sad day for me when Louie succumbed to the fly bait.

Ella: I'm so sorry to hear that, Mike. I'd never thought about the interactions between species before. I guess each individual could not get the job done on their own.

Mike: That's so true Ella, the process would not be successful without efficient teamwork. We can actually go to the "Findamicrobe" app on our phone and put up a post to secure new workers. All we do is list the jobs that need doing and wait. Usually within the day, millions of new employees are recruited and get straight to work.

Ella: Do we really need to treat wastewater? What would happen if wastewater was not treated at all? Are there any positive benefits from the biotechnological treatment of wastewater?

Mike: Great questions Ella. Yes, we definitely do need to treat wastewater. If untreated wastewater was just released back into the environment, it would be a great danger to humans, other animals, and plants. The overabundance of nutrients such as nitrogen and phosphorus can lead to deadly algal blooms. These are the rogue microbes I spoke about earlier.

As for the positive benefits, there are several beneficial by-products formed as a result of the treatment. These include biofuels, bioenergy and biofertilisers.

Ella: I had no idea about those by-products. Can you tell me more about them Mike?

Mike: Sure, biofuel, such as biodiesel, can be produced from the microalgal mass. This mass uses photosynthesis, with the aid of sunlight, to produce algal oil which in turn is converted into biodiesel. This biodiesel can then be used to power machinery and vehicles. The algal mass can also be used as biofertiliser. It's essentially algal poo. It's used by simply applying it directly to the soil. It actually has excellent water-holding properties.

In regard to bioenergy, the mixed microbial mass, or sludge if you will, metabolises the solids in the wastewater, thus maximising the amount of methane produced. The end result is a methane-rich biogas called Farticus Lotsa. This biogas can then be further processed and used as a replacement for natural gas.

Ella: So how will this environmental biotechnology minimise pollutants in the future?

Mike: As I stated earlier, the current processes reduce pollution in the environment to a manageable, safe level. This is due to the ability of the wastewater by-products to be re-purposed as fertilisers and other products. This means that there will be considerably less waste going to landfill or into the waterways. If these processes didn't occur, there would be millions more litres of harmful, untreated wastewater released into the environment.

Ella: What are some considerations for wastewater treatment going forward into the future?

Mike: To be truly effective in the future, we still need to develop more efficient strains of microbes. Crossbreeding has already begun in the labs. This must be a highly organised operation. We can't risk our microbes using "Plenty of Germs," the dating app, to find potential mates. The hook-ups must be strategically planned. This will ultimately speed up the treatment processing and reduce costs.

Some limitations for the treatment processes include environmental conditions such as temperature. Obviously, our workplace can't be air- conditioned to keep it at a constant ideal temperature. If it is too hot, the Worksafe representatives will call a stop work. All microbes on site are members of the Miscellaneous Microbe Union and must cease work when Worksafe instructs them. This, in turn, would lead to the ponds overflowing, then ultimately spewing untreated effluent into the environment.

We must all reduce our indiscriminate wasting of water. Clean water is a precious and finite resource that is a privilege. Many millions of people around the world do not have access to this basic need. I hope that I have given our listeners something to think about the next time they flush the loo or have a long shower.

Ella: Yes Mike, I'm sure we all have a better understanding of the process now. Thanks so much for talking with me today. It was very educational. You can come out from under that microscope slide now.

Mike: I'd like to thank you too Ella. You made me feel so welcome. Most people are not so keen to be in my company. If you could just pop me back into that petri dish now, I'll get Tom to take me back to the plant.

Ella: That concludes today's podcast. We hope you enjoyed hearing from Mike Robe and his wastewater enterprise. Tune in next week when I will be chatting with Professor Luna Ticke. She will be discussing if the full moon really does make us do crazy things. So, goodbye for now.

Tree of Life

by Hannah Southcott

The memorial was colourful. Sophie had insisted that each of her guests wear a different shade and, in the weeks before her death, had carefully written instructions to each of her mourners, placed them in a cheerful looking envelope, attached a stamp and left them to be posted the moment she took her last breath.

The result looked rather like a truck had smashed into a paint shop – and the canisters had carefully exploded everywhere. But that was Sophie. Never one to do anything quietly – certainly not dying.

The colours belied the depressed mood at the gathering. Memorials are seldom fun, but when someone has been taken before their time, it further dampens the mood. Sophie had lived just fifteen short years. Although to those around her, it had felt a lot longer. In a good way. More like she had always been with them, and they couldn't imagine a life without her.

But now she was gone. Forever. The bone cancer she'd been diagnosed with as a toddler had slowly claimed more and more of her frail body and finally it had swallowed her whole. Now all that was left was this horrible memorial.

Her lawyer had showed up, with a briefcase, wearing a bright pink suit. No doubt under strict instructions from her client. But why was she here?

The lawyer waited quietly at the back of the garden and when the memorial service was over, moved purposefully towards Sophie's grandma, who was weeping loudly into a floral handkerchief.

'Cynthia,' the lawyer said softly, 'I'm so sorry for your loss. I can't quite believe she's gone. Sophie was such a force of nature, I always thought...' she trailed off, unable to find the adequate words.

Grandma Cynthia loudly blew her nose and turned to look up at the tall lawyer. 'I'm sorry, I don't recall your name,' she replied rather brusquely. 'I suppose Sophie invited you, seeing as you're wearing that ghastly suit.'

She looked critically at the lawyer, who she didn't trust on principal. The lawyer was taken aback by her manner, but quickly recovered.

'Ah, my name is Angela Martin. Please call me Angela,' she said. 'Sophie told me so much about you.'

'Hmmf, well please call me Ms Ashworth, seeing as I barely know you,' Grandma Cynthia replied tartly.

'Of course,' the lawyer demurred.

'Oh, and I just remembered why you're here. To cart our Sophie off to that place so she can be liquefied,' Grandma Cynthia exclaimed. A few of the guests turned to stare in their direction. 'It's too horrible for words!'

Feeling embarrassed, the lawyer placed what she hoped was a soothing hand on Grandma Cynthia's shoulder. 'Ms Ashworth, those were Sophie's last wishes. She was very clear on her instructions.'

Grandma Cynthia sniffed her disapproval. 'I know my Sophie was eccentric, but why can't she just be buried or cremated like a normal person? This whole palaver is just too upsetting.'

The lawyer gazed around the memorial for a moment, spying Sophie's parents, who were wearing bright orange and teal and looking forlorn in the corner. 'I think you'll understand it all better once you meet the team at Eternal Tree,' she said. 'I'm not the best person to explain all the science to you. All I know is that this is what Sophie wanted.'

Grandma Cynthia scowled for a moment, then clapped her hands loudly. 'OK everyone, you've said goodbye to Sophie. Now please leave. We have to go watch our little girl be turned into mush!'

More relieved than offended, the brightly coloured crowd slowly left the garden, murmuring a few cursory farewells and condolences. Soon, only a handful of people remained, enough for perhaps half a rainbow. Sophie's parents shuffled over; grief deeply etched in the lines of their faces. A yellow-clad aunt stood under a tree, clutching a glass of water, and trying not to cry. A young boy with ancient eyes slumped on the soft cushions of the couch. A green, angular lump amongst the sea of grey.

Angela took a deep breath, aware of the hostile gazes being shot in her direction. 'I've got a letter here that Sophie wanted me to read out to you once the memorial was over,' she said. 'Can everyone hear me OK?'

There was a general nodding from all the parties, so Angela knelt down, clicked open her briefcase and withdrew a manilla envelope, which was covered in unicorn and rainbow stickers. Straightening back up, Angela took the letter from the envelope and cleared her throat.

'Dear mum and dad, Grandma Cynthia, Aunty D and Jeremy.

My lawyer is reading this to you, which means the cancer's finally got me. Please don't be too sad. Although I do expect you to cry a lot, because I was pretty amazing and you'd better all miss me like crazy.

Also please check that the lawyer is wearing a pink suit to my memorial. She'd better be. That was also one of my final wishes.

I really, really wanted to live. I think you all know that. I had so many ideas on how to save the world. I've posted them all online, so hopefully someone can find ways to actually make them work, even now I'm gone. Sometimes I wish you could see the world as I did. Nature is so magnificent, so beautiful, so splendid.

Anyway, I know you probably all find it a bit weird, but I want my body to create new life. Graveyards are full and cremation is an awful use of energy. Dying at fifteen means I can never have human children. But my body can still be used to create life. That's why I want to be in the Eternal Tree trial.

I hope you understand. Once you get there – they will explain all the details and awesome sciency stuff to you.

I love you all. Please honour my wishes or I will haunt you. Sophie xxxxxxx'

Angela's voice was thick with emotion as she read the final words. Looking around, she saw the family were smiling through their tears. It seemed that the letter had had its desired effect. Any resistance to Sophie's plans had melted away.

~~~

At 3pm, the hearse arrived to transport Sophie's body to the Eternal Tree facility. Her family bundled into a few cars, still clad in their violently vibrant attire.

When they arrived at the building – the lawyer was waiting out the front. The hearse was directed through a boom-gate off to the side – and presumably, Sophie's body would be transferred there. The family disembarked from their vehicles and the small group gathered and then waited for the glass doors to open. Inside, they were greeted by a youthful looking man with dark hair and smooth olive skin.

'Welcome,' he said with a slight lilt. 'I'm Gideon Halpert and I'm the founder of Eternal Tree. You must be Sophie's family. She was a truly wonderful person and we're honoured she chose us, to assist her in her next stage of life.'

Grandma Cynthia glared at him. 'She's dead,' she said firmly. 'There is no next stage of life.'

The man smiled a little awkwardly, then continued. 'That really depends on your definition of life. For us here at Eternal Tree, we know that all life is made of atoms. These atoms have been in countless different forms before they became a human form, and will be in countless forms after.'

Grandma Cynthia rolled her eyes and snorted. 'Can you please just tell us what it is you do here?'

The young man smiled again and this time it reached his eyes. 'If you'll bear with me a few moments more, I'd love to explain everything,' he said. 'I don't know if any of you have been to a cemetery recently?'

The lawyer and Sophie's parents nodded.

'Well, cemeteries are often huge, in most countries in the world, cemeteries are full to over- flowing. They are a bit of a wasteland of stones and weeds. So, I wanted to offer an alternative to being buried in such a depressing place. Somewhere the family can still visit and remember.'

He paused for a moment, looking around. 'I have a degree in microbiology. So, this project is my little effort to try and help the community and the environment at the same time. Basically, we have a method that utilises microbes to break down human bodies into a sort of nutrient soup. We capture any gases released and store them to use a fuel. We then plant the seed of a forest tree – which has been carefully selected by the client. We grow the seed, feeding it the nutrient soup, until it is ready to be planted. Eternal Tree currently has three planting zones, but we plan on having many more in the future. The tree planting usually takes place around a year after the person passes away. The tree is cared for by a full-time caretaker, but we've also found that family members love to weed and water the tree. Over time, the forest grows and instead of a barren, rocky wasteland, it becomes a beautiful, living memorial. But it's more than that, it's also a place of biodiversity and life, a piece of nature that families can enjoy for generations to come. Instead of cutting down trees to bury people, we're planting them.'

The family looked at him, a stunned expression on their faces. 'I'm happy to answer any questions you might have,' he said.

Grandma Cynthia recovered her composure first. 'Why don't you just cremate people? We did that with my Great Aunt Doris and popped it in a pot and grew the most beautiful roses. Why do you have to turn them into a soup?'

Gideon turned to the formidable lady and realised, despite her combative stance, she was in fact quite a tiny woman and clad entirely in green.

'Cremation requires a huge amount of energy. For a human body to be reduced to ash, it must be burnt at nearly 2000 degrees for two to three hours. It also emits a significant amount of carbon. The ash produced can be put in a pot-plant, sure.'

There was a slight cough from the man in orange, who must have been Sophie's father. He said, softly, 'I think it's rather a splendid idea. What tree did Sophie choose? And where exactly are you going to plant it?'

'I'm glad you asked,' Gideon said, turning to the man. 'Sophie chose a Rosewood or *Dysoxylum fraserianum*. It's a rainforest tree which is native to this part of the country and as it matures provides important habitat for a number of plant and animal species. And just like Sophie, it's a fairly tough tree. Drought resistant, able to grow in a wide range of soils and salt and frost tolerant.'

The family were nodding now and there was a flicker of a smile on the mother's face.

'Eternal Tree has purchased an old dairy farm about 10 kilometres north from here,' he continued. 'The soil is quite degraded, but we have a team of microbiologists, mycologists and soil experts working to prepare it for its future as a forest. If you come with me, I have a map of our different plantation sites.'

The family trooped after Gideon, gazing at the strange fungi photos that lined the walls. They entered a huge round room, with a tree growing in the centre. Part of the glass ceiling was open.

'That's my grandmother,' Gideon said quietly. 'It's a wattle, with brilliant yellow flowers – a show- stopper, just like she was. She was my first customer. She hated the idea of being in a cemetery, but she loved the idea of becoming part of a forest'.

There was a large table near the tree – with a digital map of the town. Three areas were highlighted bright green. Gideon pointed to the locations and explained some of the reasoning behind choosing them.

He then led them through to the nursery – where dozens of seedlings were growing in small pots. 'Once these seedlings are a few months old, we transplant them with the nutrient soup. We grow them for about a year, constantly monitoring and feeding them and working to establish beneficial fungi in the organic matter to give them the best chance of survival once they are planted in the soil.'

The young boy with the ancient eyes now spoke up. 'How long does it take to turn a human body into soup?' he asked. 'How soon before Sophie becomes part of one of these trees?'

Brushing his hands softly over the leaves of one sapling, Gideon replied, 'The process varies a little from person to person. We utilise the body's natural microbes as well as additional ones to help the body decompose. Generally, it takes two to three months.'

The boy nodded. 'How do the saplings respond once they are fed the soup?'

Gideon chuckled, 'Oh they really take off then, it's usually a significant growth spurt, you can almost see them growing. The nutrient soup is like a very rich multivitamin.'

He continued his tour, taking them down a corridor to a steel door. Punching in a code and presenting his fingerprint, he then led them into another warehouse sized room. It was divided into two sections. They were behind a thick pane of glass – on the other side it looked like an indoor garden, but with strange-coloured containers. There were trees, shrubs, plants, and mushrooms growing around these containers. The ceiling was glass, but it was securely closed.

There appeared to be a web-like sprinkler system attached to it. There was a whirr of huge extraction fans.

'This is where the decomposition takes place,' Gideon said, motioning to the coloured containers. 'We've found it best to keep the process as natural as possible. The bodies emit gases as they break down, which are captured by these extraction fans. The flora provides any additional microbes that are needed.'

'It looks peaceful,' murmured Grandma Cynthia.

Ushering the family along, the group were soon back in the lobby and seated on a comfortable couch, with tea, coffee, and a good selection of biscuits.

'Can we come and see her here?' Sophie's mother asked, her voice catching on her words.

Gideon nodded. 'You have to make an appointment, but yes, you can visit here in the first three months. Once Sophie is merged with the tree, we move the sapling to the growing location, while it's still small, so it can acclimatise there.'

There was silence as the family glanced at each other.

'And the planting?' Sophie's father inquired. 'Can we be there when she's planted?' Six pairs of anxious eyes flickered onto Gideon's face.

'Of course,' Gideon replied. 'Our team will work with you to organise a mutually beneficial time and date for the planting, and we encourage family to be a part of it. After she's been planted, you are free to visit as often as you wish. We even have a volunteer program for families who want to become more involved in caring for the forest as it grows.'

A year later, Angela, Grandma Cynthia and Sophie's parents stood around as her tree was planted.

The boy with the ancient eyes had died a few months earlier, inevitably succumbing to the cancer ravaging his small body. He'd asked for the spot next to Sophie, so the two of them could finally grow up together. The Tallowwood sapling would be planted there the following spring.

A large, deep hole had been bored into the soil and the family and lawyer watched as it was partially filled with fertilisers, composts, and wood chips. The rosewood sapling was carefully lowered into the hole and the remaining soil was thrown in and carefully compacted. The tree looked happy, healthy, full of life.

As she gazed at the skinny limbs and vibrant green leaves, Grandma Cynthia thought she could see something of Sophie there, that gangly girl who had brought so much joy everywhere she went. Perhaps in this body, she'd have a chance to grow, to experience the seasons, to provide shade and shelter for generations to come. A place of life and hope, even after death.

She smiled and stroked the smooth bark of the tree, whispering, 'I'll be here every week to make sure you're going strong my girl. This time you'll outlive us all.'

What Any Fool Can Do

by Vienna O'Shea

The flight landed at a run-down airport that managed to appear both frozen and dusty at the same time. Only a few passengers disembarked from the small plane. A new jeep, shiny with chrome, was waiting to take him on the long drive to site. Although the road was made up, its surface was rutted, limiting the vehicle's speed; but the driver seemed steady and serious. The oil company provided good wages and training, and other jobs would be hard to come by here. Occasional headlights threaded the route in the opposite direction, but there was hardly any traffic. Despite the midwinter season, little snow lay on the ground: any type of precipitation was rare in this region, and what fell now would be carried away by the shrieking winds across a thousand kilometres of open tundra.

He reached the camp a couple of hours later, as evening darkness thickened into night. A young man showed him into the guest accommodation - like everything else on site, it looked like a portacabin, but was well insulated and comfortable inside. After a quick shower, he joined his hosts in the canteen. The food was excellent: not just tasty, but high-class restaurant quality. "You'd soon get complaints if you served mush here - people work six weeks on, and there isn't much else to look forward to at the end of the day". He was invited to watch this evening's screening of a classic cowboy film, but politely declined in favour of sleep. He was probably getting too old for this type of visit: yet there was always something fascinating about troubleshooting real problems. And it might mean more funding for his team, and a chance to test out their new bioremediation technology on a real site.

Next morning started early, with meetings on the proposed bioremediation strategy. He briefly summarised what they had already heard, trying to emphasise the potential of this innovative approach. His hosts were courteous, but perhaps deliberately bland and non-committal. People left and rejoined the meeting as urgent business came up elsewhere.

At 10:30, coffee and biscuits were brought in - hardly needed, after a full breakfast just a few hours ago. Then they moved out to inspect the damaged area of the site.

The process of suiting up for the visit was at once familiar and not. All sites had safety protocols and protective equipment, and from his experience there would be a strict routine and route: no-one was going to let you wander unescorted around a live production facility. But in this case, there was the added factor of the outside temperature. Without proper clothing, survival times in that harsh cold would not be long: so the boiler suits were heavily insulated, with deep fur-edging on the hoods, and the outfit included thermal boots. All the clothing was bright scarlet, to increase the chances of a rescue team finding people quickly if they were injured or became disorientated and wandered off in a rare blizzard. By the time they were suited up, he looked and felt like a giant version of one of his granddaughter's beloved puffy toys...

The damaged area was much as he'd expected. Many years previously a plume of gas and oil had sprayed out, contaminating the sandy soil. The challenge was in the extremely dry and cold conditions: although it was decades ago, the surface still looked like a piece of moonscape within that already-barren land. Remediation was required under the updated site licence, and he could see this would be a perfect test ground for the new techniques his team was pioneering.

The tour didn't include the main production site, but he'd seen the promotional video and had visited plenty like it before. They called in briefly at the laboratory block, another set of portacabins housing state-of-the-art equipment for soils testing. That could be useful if they got the bioremediation contract. On the way back, a debate sprang up between his guides. One asked if he would like to see the wastewater treatment plant; another said what for, and anyway it would make them late for lunch. An expression of interest on his part was enough to settle it. As a young engineer, he'd started in wastewater treatment and had only moved on to soil bioremediation later in his career. And after all, the second guide assured him, there were always chefs on duty to rustle up a cordon bleu snack for staff and visitors. He wondered a little at the things needed to motivate us, out in this vast, austere wilderness.

The wastewater plant only took domestic sewage, but the camp was the size of a small town, and another condition for working in this territory was to provide on-site treatment of any wastes before removal. It looked like a standard package plant, a large olive-green tank with flanged steel pipes weaving in and out of it, though the manufacturer's name was unfamiliar. The wastewater would first enter a primary sedimentation chamber for solids to settle out in the quiescent conditions; then to another chamber for secondary biological treatment; then into a secondary sedimentation tank to recover the microbial biomass and discharge clarified water. After that, the operator told him, the flow passed on to a sand filter and a chlorination unit before testing and discharge to a storage pond. In a dry region like this, it seemed a pity not to re-use the treated water for irrigation somewhere on site: but maybe that could become part of the soil bioremediation project.

Standing on top of the package plant, the production site looked like a charcoal drawing, the tall gantries and pipework silver-grey against the snow-coloured sky. He asked the operator how the treatment process was performing. "Not too well - I've tried adjusting things on the package plant, but we aren't meeting our standards and it puts all the downstream units out. I've told them we may need to buy a new one." Ordering a new plant seemed a drastic solution: the manufacturer's price would be nothing for an oil company, but the cost of shipping, customs clearance, storage and transport to this remote area would soon add up. It was worth asking more questions.

The operator showed him where flow from the accommodation blocks, kitchens, and on-site showers and toilets entered a pump well, then was lifted up to the package plant by a submersible pump. The original pump had been replaced before he'd been given the job of running the plant, but the only way he could make things work was to let the pump well fill and allow wastewater to back up through the sewer system, then run the pump in a 10-minute burst. The backing up didn't seem to be a problem: there was almost a kilometre of sewer pipe back to the site, with plenty of storage capacity.

He asked the operator how often the pump was switched on. "Oh, once a day - that's enough to empty the sewers." Once a day? Together they looked at the pump rating, then he asked a few more questions - about the size of the sewer pipe, and the number of people on site. The package plant was a sealed unit, and he declined an eager offer to find spanners for the bolts on the inspection hatch: but the two of them lifted the lid off the sand filter, which appeared curiously empty of sand. The others, standing on top of the package plant in the sharp wind, looked bored and cold. He thanked the operator and they returned to the warm office block.

Next day in the briefing room he outlined what he had learned from the site visit. Testing would be needed to identify the best process parameters and micro-organisms to carry out the bioremediation: an expensive option, but still far less costly than transporting soil a thousand kilometres for treatment elsewhere. He remembered one of his university lecturers saying, "An Engineer is someone who can do for one dollar what any fool can do for two." At the time he was young and idealistic, wanting to save the planet, and this definition hadn't pleased him. But the older he got, the more truth he felt there was in it, and he was tempted to re-cast it for the 21st century. Because $1 (or €, £, ¥ or whatever) was simply a measure of resource; and if you could do something with half the resources then the other half would be left to tackle another problem...

Questions on the bioremediation proposal were beginning to wind down. After a brief pause, he added, "And I can fix your wastewater plant." The audience stirred slightly: some senior managers probably hadn't realised there was a problem, or that he knew about it. But they seemed prepared to listen.

"You are planning to bring in a new package plant which will probably cost upwards of a quarter of a million, all told. But this is how the plant is being operated at present." He briefly outlined the problem: the total flow was passing through in a matter of minutes, with no chance for anything to settle; and the beneficial micro-organisms were simply being washed out of the system. "It's not just a mechanical process - the microbes are at the heart of it, and the whole biological treatment depends entirely on them." He stopped for breath, and to let that sink in. "And on top of that, your sand filter isn't working properly as all the sand has been washed away. So when you take samples from the outlet and send them off for analysis, you are pretty well seeing what went into the plant, without any treatment having occurred at all."

He paused again, this time for effect. "All you actually need to do is buy a smaller pump. That way the flow rate will match the tank size and the biology can get on and do its work."

There was a moment of silence while they considered it, then a voice piped up: "What about the sand filter? Doesn't it need specially graded sand and...?" He almost snorted: someone had obviously learned something about wastewater treatment at college but wasn't thinking. "What about those sieves in your geotechnical labs? Don't waste thousands shipping the right grade of sand here - this place is practically a desert. Just use the equipment you have to grade your own."

He drew another breath. "And while you are at it, the guy who runs the treatment plant seems to have some common sense: why not give him some training on how biological wastewater treatment really works? A bit of kit in the corner of the Geotechnical lab and he can do basic tests here on site. You'll save time and money on flying routine samples hundreds of miles to the nearest lab and get answers back much more quickly. If he's any good, he may even be able to help with the bioremediation monitoring."

The meeting broke up, after a few more technical questions on the bioremediation concept. A quick lunch, with some warm but desultory conversation on everyday topics. He thanked his hosts, who thanked him: then the jeep was ready to take him back to the little airport - another vehicle, another driver, the same long featureless road. He caught the plane with just enough time to pass through security, and on arrival at the main airport transferred to the international section. An hour or so in the large, dimly lit departure lounge writing up his notes, then soon after the jet was climbing away with the lights of the snow-bound city twinkling below him. He slept.

Next afternoon in the office, an email popped into the inbox. It thanked him for his time, hoped he had found the visit useful - and requested that his team proceed with submitting the detailed proposal and full costing for a trial of the new bioremediation technique. A final sentence said, "We are also grateful for your useful comments on the site's wastewater treatment facility and will be adopting your proposed solution." He smiled, and it was the smile of a satisfied professional.

Sorrows in the Sediments

by Dolly Joy O. Ogatis

I have heard many stories about the world we cannot see. A world elusive, unforgiving, but beautiful nonetheless. A flawless replica of our own. Only that its inhabitants are much smaller, molecular, and smarter.

"Amanda, I'm sorry for your loss." I stared blankly at the elderly woman who spoke. Words tangled up in my tongue. I don't know how to respond to her. My eyes built a mind of their own that my tears trickled; unstoppable. I can no longer feel my body until someone pulled me into a tight embrace. Only then I freed my sobs to life, rocking my body against someone else's.

Sorrows have become a fundamental part of my life. Loss and isolation have only added insult to injury. Should I ask for more?

I lost my mother that morning from the flood. And her body is still unfound. I am the survivor, they said. Or, that is what they wanted me to believe.

"We know it is hard for you right now, but you need to come to the shelter with us. This area is destroyed. There's nothing much left for you to hold on to and stay here, dear." One of the community shepherds advised. They mean well, and I understand that. But this *area* is what I call home. It has been me and my mother's home.

"It must have been a great trauma for the girl." I hear another voice spoke as I clutch a worn-out bag where my clothes once were.

The coastal flood took lives that morning. From the evening before, the town officials had warned us about a storm from the Pacific. The night before the coastal flood, my mother and I tried to cover our home with salvaged tarps. We secured the chickens in their cages and made sure the nets and posts were sturdy enough to hold the ponds. We thought the storm would only pass by and all would be well the next morning. We thought wrong.

The town had suffered a great loss. The storm had crippled the community. Many families have lost their loved ones, including me. I cannot quite remember how I lost my mother that morning. My memory was fogged with ...trauma. My brain refused to remember, and my heart refused to yield.

All I can recall and told the authorities was something that involved waves. Crashing waves. Muddy and strong. It destroyed everything in its wake. The authorities told us that the coastal flood was brought by the typhoon, but they did not tell us one thing. The mangroves are dying from oil spills, and the flash flood was the consequence. A lot of people do not know, but I do.

I let them drag me to the shelter like a tethered goat. News, filtered and unfiltered, flew by from one tongue to another as I huddled up in the corner and listened. I heard of the devastating news of the mangrove forest near where we live. I heard of some Teddy who went missing. That name rings a bell. I think I knew him from school. For the most part, I sulk. I could no longer cry or weep. I turned myself into a mute.

For the rest of the world, time did not pause. Months have passed and some families have found their dead. I never found mine. A few bodies were recovered near the estuary, greenbelts, and the coastline. Mostly dead.

Carcasses stretched to the horizon. I watched the rescuers huddle up dead bodies, placed them in dark bags and zipped them up. I must have been hallucinating for I could see souls floating near the corpses. Their sorrow echoing from beneath the coastal waters as if it was buried deep in the sediments.

While the rest of the world moved on, I saw myself moving backwards. I found my place under the wing of one of the caretakers of the mangrove forest, Aunt Luzviminda – a close relative. I refused to become a burden, so I worked as a mangrove forest ranger. I guarded the post in the mangrove ranger station and, sometimes, I roved the mangrove forest by the pump boat.

I kept coming back to the forest, searching...

Peace and solace enveloped me as I cruised through the firth with only the sound of the incessant rotor and the birds chirping coming in one syncing chorale through the wind. Breeding birds took shelter within the mangrove roots. The marine life thrumming beneath them.

Life in the mangrove forest was nothing new. I grew up near the coastline and the greenbelts. My mother and I sold chickens and *tilapia*, grown from our own pond, for a living. Now all of that remained only as memories.

The sky was bleak, with clouds reckoning storm. As I rounded up through the winding waterways, the sight of another boat came into view. Located only a few metres away, the boat looked bigger than mine, newer.

A guy, donning a tawny drawstring hat, leaned unfashionably over the boat to reach down to the waters with a vial in his hand. He drew up the vial filled with coastal waters. He did it again with more vials. He must have been so engrossed with his work that he had not noticed the sound of another pump boat closing in.

From where I was, I could see him collecting the coastal waters like he was playing. He looked more like a frolicking child, rather than an adult doing serious work.

"Hey!" I called out and waved.

He had just finished closing up another vial as he spun around to see me. I waved again. "Do you need some help?" I asked out loud. I did not know the reason why I asked, but I asked.

Although he waved back, he turned around and went to secure the vial. His boat roared to life again and he drove towards where I was. A cordial smile took form on his mouth.

"Hi! I'm Mathew. Nice to meet you."

"Amanda." The distance between our boats was too wide for us to mind for a handshake. "Are you with the research team? Do you need some help?"

"Ah yes. I was with them a while ago, until I wandered out here. I might need some help going back to the coast." He grinned.

"Well, in that, I can surely help you."

I manoeuvred my boat back to the path I took and tilted my head at Mathew; telling him to follow along. When we reached the estuary, I said, "The coastline was right over there. I guess you know your way back from the beach."

"Yes. Thank you," he said. I nodded politely and was ready to leave when he spoke again. "Uh, Amanda? I might need to take some more samples tomorrow, too. Maybe you could help me find better locations in the forest. You seem like an expert at navigating the mangrove forest. I could really use some help."

"Sure. Tell me where to meet and what time."

Mathew looked around. "Here, at six in the morning. Would that be, okay?"

"Absolutely. See you tomorrow, then."

The next morning came. I knew I was on time, but Mathew was already waiting at our rendezvous which made me ask, "Am I late?"

Mathew grinned, "No. I'm just earlier."

Mathew turned out to be a student researcher who was assisting his professor in a research collaboration. That means he was a bit older than me.

"We're taking environmental samples. Coastal waters, soil, sediments, samples from the roots of those *Rhizophora*, you name it. I take everything I can find," he said.

"All for what?" I asked.

"For research. We heard this community had suffered great losses due to a storm a year ago. We're here to help."

"You think you can help us with your research?"

He closed the vial and heaved a sigh. "We conduct research to help. But sometimes, not all researches can yield favorable results, you know. What we're doing here is still without certainty. But that's what makes research even more exhilarating and interesting. If you know what you're doing then it's not called research, is it?" he paused. "Are you one of the survivors?" He asked in a careful tone.

I nodded. "What is your research about?"

"We're studying the unique microbiome of this ecosystem. Trying to fully understand the microbe-mangrove relationship and interaction so we could draw some conclusions on how to better take care of this ecosystem and the wide variety of life depending on it."

I held his gaze on me. "Tell me more."

"Well," he cleared his throat. "This ecosystem protects the coastal life and the life in the terrains. The disaster that happened here a year ago is a clear sign that the mangrove forest is deteriorating due to the oil spill." Mathew looked around to take in the greens and blues of our surroundings. Shortly, his eyes went back to me. "We need to save this place now more than ever." "I see that you care a lot, even though you're not from here."

"I don't have to live here to see nature's worth, Amanda."

"If your research will yield excellent results, what then?"

"We'll use it for bioremediation. The level of oil spill here is decreasing now that we have deployed microorganisms that could metabolize oil. Another problem was how could we plant more mangroves annually. That's why we're trying to study the relationship between mangroves and its microbiome. See if we could find microorganisms that could promote better growth."

"What kind of microorganisms are you after?"

"We're looking for certain endophytes which can be a source of bioactive compounds that promote plant health and growth. They're collectively called PGPB."

"PGPB? What does that mean?"

"Plant growth promoting bacteria," he answered. "We can use them for a more successful mangrove reforestation, hence mangrove conservation and rehabilitation. We're protecting the environment in our own small way, with the help of our little, invisible friends. Hoping that what occurred a year ago won't happen again."

Recollection of events from a year ago stirred up. I drew in a strained breath as I force the treacherous tears back.

"Are you okay?" Mathew asked. Concern marred his eyes.

"I just remembered some things."

He was quick to ask, "Did I say something to trigger that?"

"Somehow," I croaked. "I lost my mother in that flood. The rescuers were never able to recover her body. I watched other dead bodies get rescued, recovered straight from the mud. Their families crouching over them, mourning. At least they had something to mourn on. At least they saw the ones they lost. I was never able to do that," I said. I looked at Mathew and for the first time in my life I saw genuine sympathy.

"I'm very sorry," he said in a quiet voice.

I shook my head, putting off the sorrows creeping in. "Our house was destroyed by the flood. It was located nearby. I kept coming back here more than I used to after the disaster. Perhaps because I was looking for my missing piece. People tell me I was supposed to go out there, move on, but I find myself limping my way back here."

"Have you done anything else other than see the mangroves and cruise around the forest?" Mathew asked.

I shook my head.

"Why don't you come to the house tomorrow?"

I frown at his suggestion.

"I can show you what we're working on. At least parts of it. Most of the work is back at the university. If you'd like, we can mess around with a few specimens or samples that we can retrieve here."

"Will that be okay?"

"Yeah. Professor Dianne is kind and she's out of town. Most of the team is out in the morning. Nothing to worry about, plus, you will be the one to take your own sample and view it under the microscope tomorrow. Sounds fun, no?"

For some reason, my heart thumped at the anticipation of tomorrow's excitement. It could have been the reason for my impulsive agreement to Mathew.

The next morning, we found ourselves a new rendezvous. The house was located at the west side of the shore. I docked my boat near the wooden boardwalk and trudged my way through white sands;

Hermit crabs skittering beneath my feet. Mathew was waiting by the front door, hands shoved into his pockets. He opened the door for me and gestured inside.

"Welcome to our humble lab house," he said. "Here is your personally collected sample from yesterday." He handed a vial to me. The house looked normal from the outside, yet it was completely different inside.

The living room was furnished with white benches replacing the typical chairs and sofas. Microscopes lined up the tabletops and some other dishes were sprawled over them. I ran my eyes over the scribblings on the large whiteboard. They were not nonsensical scribblings. They were numbers, computations, and drawings coupled with arrows.

"I suppose the whiteboard is your TV replacement?" I quipped. Mathew chuckled.

"This place is amazing," I said.

"Uh-uh. Amazing things happen here too." He turned one microscope on and told me to come close. "Here. Place a drop of your sample in this glass slide, and we'll see what you've got."

I followed his instructions deliberately. He instructed me to cover the slide with a cover slip. It was small, thin glass. I thought I would break it if I was not careful enough.

"You've got steady hands," he said. I took that as a compliment. "Hold that slide and clip that on this platform." I did what he said. Once clipped, he asked me to move to the opposite side of the microscope. I followed suit as Mathew placed his eyes on the binoculars at his side of the microscope. My eyes were awkwardly adjusting with the binoculars.

At first, I just saw white. But Mathew was making a few adjustments with the lenses before an image morphed into its complete form.

"What is this?" I asked.

"You mean, what are these?" When I removed my eyes from the binoculars, Mathew was grinning. He told me to return to my binoculars and started explaining what each weird moving form was. He told me the green ones were probably *cyanobacteria*. He mentioned some amoeba as well. He pointed out some algae and nematodes. A few scientific names were mentioned, but my attention was no longer on his words. I was too fascinated at how much life a single drop of water could harbor.

"Come here, let me show you something more interesting."

He led me to another room. The weirdest room, with the weirdest bottles and equipment. "Those bottles are called Winogradsky Columns. We place them near the window to allow photosynthesis to occur inside the column and let our photosynthetic friends thrive."

"What are they for?"

"We use them as our source for microorganisms intended for enrichment culture. Those columns can last for months."

Mathew walked me through weirder but more fascinating stuff. Although calling them all "stuff" doesn't do them justice. They are full of purpose and wonder.

That day ended, but the happiness in my heart did not fade away. The memory kept repeating in my head like a broken record. That experience brought freedom to my soul. The rigor of the study, the triumph that can come from discovery, and the vision of a better future with research. There was so much to be done, and somehow, I start to notice the wonder of the elusive and the unseen.

Mathew and I did not meet for the next few days, since I had to work and he has to go back to the university. We were not able to say our formal goodbyes, even.

The days stretched on until it turned into months. Aunty Luzviminda told me that my college life is long overdue and it's time for me to go back to school again. She convinced me to take the scholarship examination in our town. Luckily, I passed. It was large enough for me to attend a university in a nearby city and pursue biology.

I came home every once in a while, mostly by the end of every semester. And three years later, I found myself cruising back to the mangrove forest, aboard a new and bigger boat. Along with me are the proper tools I will be needing for sample collection and transport.

I crossed the estuary and reached the greenbelt's waterways. The mangrove forest now thicker and denser. The sweet call of the starling coaxed me to close my eyes for a moment. When I opened them again, the greener surroundings, the bluer sky, and a life livelier than before stared back.

That day, I took samples from six different locations. By the time the horizon was a splash of bright red and orange skies, I reached the estuary. I stopped the boat and looked back to the coastal greenbelts. To the one I called home.

I thought sorrows were all that I could find in these sediments. But the deeper I wonder, the louder life echoes. The life of a world within our world. An invisible world where a million stories await to unfold. Thus, my quest is yet to begin.

From the Ashes

Elizabeth Taylor

A mit sat, cross-legged, on the floor. His posture stiff, back held straight, he ignored the growing tickle in his throat from the cough that had troubled him for years. Periodically, his gaze travelled between the door and the kurta on the mat in front of him. Even in the dim light, the shirt's maroon silk shone, an otherworldly glow in such a setting, like a jewel in a pile of waste.

He'd thought as much the moment he'd unwrapped it last month – even when his wife assured him that a street vendor had slashed its price, given her an offer she couldn't resist, especially with his birthday only a week away. He knew better now. Through a series of casual enquiries over the last two weeks, he knew exactly how much the finely embroidered fabric had cost the family, in much more than just its price tag.

He waited for the door to open while his wife prepared their evening meal over the chulha. Woodsmoke, a thick blanket of sulphuric tendrils, filled the air between them.

Priyanka worked in silence; their blazing row had exhausted their words. Now the only flame came from the chulha. In the small room, each ambient sound seemed magnified: monsoon rains hissed on the tin roof, the fire cracked and popped, and each fresh ingredient

Priyanka added to the kadai – chilli, onion, cumin seeds – spat and shrieked.

The door swung open. His fifteen-year-old daughter stepped in from under a large umbrella – new? – and turned her back to Amit while she dropped her school bag and closed the umbrella. At the sight of Diya's uniform, a light blue striped shirt and grey skirt, the biggest expense at the school, Amit's nostrils flared. He glowered at her back, waiting for her to turn, aware that Priyanka's bustling motions had also stalled, since she too was no doubt staring at their only daughter.

Diya turned and her usual smile faltered as her gaze flittered across the room and settled on the kurta. Her thick eyebrows furrowed.

'Care to explain where this kurta came from, beti?' Amit controlled his tone, keeping it light.

'Mammii bought…' Diya trailed off and Amit glimpsed Priyanka shaking her head in his periphery vision.

'Mammii lied,' he stated. A throbbing pulse grew at his temple. 'I know exactly how much this cost *and* how you came into so much money.'

Diya dropped to her knees. 'Paapaa, it's a good thing. Surely you see?' She lifted the kurta and held it to him like an offering. 'With my wage, we can afford nice things. We don't have to live like this –'

He snatched the kurta and screwed it up, throwing it against a bare wall. 'We live like this *for* you. Every rupee I've ever earned I've used to pay the fees for your school.'

'And I'm grateful, paapaa,' she cried. 'I know how hard you work. But the school is no good!'

Amit sucked in a breath. 'No good? What do you mean, no good?'

She hung her head. 'I am sorry, Paapaa. I pretended to like it because –'

Amit flinched. He got to his feet and turned away from her as his daughter continued to spin her lies.

'– I wanted you to be happy. But it really is no good! It is obvious now I am not there. I have learnt more English in the last month than I ever did at that school, and –'

'Enough!' he roared, swinging back to her. 'I have heard enough. All you do is pour lie upon lie. First, you lie to me about your whereabouts and get a job at *that* place. Then you conspire with your mother to hide this from me for over a month. You parade around in your school uniform each day while you laugh at me and the money I waste on your education behind my back.'

'No, Paapaa, it wasn't like that. We just didn't know how to tell –'

'Silence! Now you are caught, you further lie by trying to pretend your school was no good, when really, all you care about is taking dirty money from the same people who took –' He broke off as he struggled to catch his breath and the hacking cough returned. 'I vowed,' he wheezed when he could, tears blurring his vision, 'I vowed that I would never again accept so much as a paisa from these so-called 'recycling' centres. And it will be over my dead body that my daughter makes the same mistake.'

He pointed to the open doorway into the only other room in the house, where their two small beds perched on bricks in case of flooding. 'Go to bed,' he said.

'Paapaa, please.'

'Go!' He grabbed her arms and dragged her up.

Suddenly, Priyanka was tugging at his arms. 'You go too far, Amit! She's not a little girl anymore.'

He swung his shaking arm from his daughter to the doorway. 'Go! You will stay there until I've had time to sort out this mess. And you,' he snarled at Priyanka, 'you will ensure she stays there while I am out tomorrow.'

Diya wiped her tear-streaked face and backed away into the other room without another word.

Amit coughed into his arm for several minutes.

When he recovered, Priyanka was glaring at him with her hands on her hips. 'It won't bring him back, you know,' she said in a low voice.

Amit held up his hands. 'We're not having this conversation.' 'Then we won't have any conversation.'

Priyanka resumed her work at the chulha, rolling chapatis with quick, sharp movements. When she placed the food between them, Amit ate methodically without tasting a thing that entered his mouth. Priyanka layered fish masala and rice, sweet from being boiled in local sugar cane juice, onto chapati, which she delivered, without a word, to the other room. On her return, he caught her eye, and she sniffed theatrically as she stooped to pick up and straighten the kurta.

~~~

Under Diya's umbrella, Amit paused on the road outside the new 'recycling' plant and scrunched his face. If he ignored the gleaming white paint job, the place didn't look all that much different from the paper mill where he had worked when he first arrived in Muzaffarnagar thirteen years ago. Within the sprawling complex jutted cylindrical shapes that must be chimneys, though he couldn't see any smoke. Counting at least eight of them, he spat onto the road slicked with rainwater.

One chimney was more than enough. A chimney meant a furnace. And it meant that somewhere inside an ignorant young man, lured by the promise of a higher wage than in the countryside, was hauling bits of plastic fragments into the fire, a cheap source of fuel to power the industry.

One by one, the paper and sugar mills had been closed for violations to public health in the mid-2020s, and the air had been cleaner in the last five years. But that was already too late for Amit's family. And the new plant towered over Amit now, ready to envelop the city in a fresh haze of toxic smog.

His cough dislodged a cascade of bullet-like water droplets from the umbrella, prompting him to move. He marched into the site, located the reception area, and strode to the desk, umbrella under arm like a bayonet.

'I'm here to terminate my daughter's employment,' he said. 'Her name is Diya Mathur.'

'Just a moment, sir.' The girl at the desk, who looked about Diya's age, rattled a keyboard. She frowned at a slim computer screen for a moment. 'A thousand apologies, sir, but there is no way for this to be done.'

'What do you mean? I am her father and I want her off your books.'

'According to our records, Diya is fifteen, yes?'

He nodded.

'This means she is legally entitled to work here, sir, in which case we need a formal letter of resignation, and she must work a notice period of thirty days as is outlined in her contract. I can print off a copy of her contract for you to read if that would help, sir?'

Was that a smirk as the girl delivered her final 'sir'?

The throbbing in his temple returned. He dropped the umbrella on the desk and leaned over it. 'Now, see here, I am her father, and I will not have her work in a place like this! You call this a 'recycling' plant, but I know it's all a sham. You care about nothing but profit, and your 'recycling' amounts to nothing more than –'

'What is going on here?'

Amit turned to the intruder, a man in a white lab coat, who had stepped up beside him. Though he sported a stubbly beard and spoke authoritatively, Amit thought he was probably at least ten years his junior, somewhere in his late twenties. His expressive features, as he listened to Amit's demands, radiated a kind of energy that life had long since zapped from Amit. A swinging lanyard branded him as Dr Rahul Uppal.

'Come,' he said, 'let's talk this out over tea.'

When they settled in an office – as big as Amit's entire home – with hot drinks steaming between them, Dr Uppal said, 'I'm curious to know what type of recycling plant you think this is, Mr Mathur.'

'Paper, presumably.' There'd been talk aplenty about the plant during its construction, but Amit hadn't been able to bring himself to listen; he'd walked away from anyone who raised it. They were all fools, gullible fools.

'A logical guess,' Dr Uppal said, 'given Muzaffarnagar's recent history. But we are here to recycle plastics, Mr Mather.'

Amit snorted. 'Most plastics can't be recycled. It gets burned.'

At the mill, he had spent some time as a picker, sifting through the huge import of plastic waste that 'accidentally' came in with the mixed papers for recycling from far away countries like America. Only a fraction of it, like plastic bottles, was deemed 'valuable' and the rest of it had ended up in a furnace somewhere or other.

Dr Uppal shook his head. 'That may have been true a decade ago, but the world of plastic recycling has come a long way since then.' He sipped his tea. 'Take this plant, for instance. This is a *bio*recycling plant, based on a model first built in France in 2025. In those days, only one type of plastic could be biorecycled. Here, however, we deal with five main types of plastics, and I can assure you that none are ever burned, even those we can't yet biodegrade.' He placed his empty cup on its saucer and gave Amit a warm smile. 'I'd love to show you around, show you how it works.'

Amit lifted his own cup, taking slow sips. The young doctor seemed earnest, but Amit knew he had no way of knowing for sure. Perhaps seeing more of the plant would be a good idea: if they were burning here, he would see evidence of it somewhere. While he finished his tea, he asked Rahul about his background. The young doctor had studied at the Indian Institute of Science in Bangalore, worked abroad for several years at the French biorecycling plant, and took a managerial role at this new plant that had brought him back to India last year.

'I dream of a world where no plastic ends up as waste,' he told Amit. 'Come, let me show you our work.'

Rahul guided Amit through the stages of plastic recycling, carefully explaining the various scientific processes in simple terms. Some of the cylindrical bodies Amit had mistaken for chimneys turned out to be huge vats, in which the factory cultured enzymes from the guts of microscopic organisms that could actually eat plastic. 'Enzymes are like tiny scissors,' Rahul told him. 'They cut the plastics into tiny pieces, called monomers, which can be put back together to form new plastics.'

In one hall, deliveries of plastic bales were arriving on forklifts.

'All the plastic here originates in Uttar Pradesh,' Rahul said. 'Long gone are the days when rich countries would export their waste to suffocate poorer countries. Most plastic recycling is done at regional level these days, and we're hoping to replicate this across India by 2040.'

Other plastics arrived on the backs of waste pickers. Surprised, Amit exchanged a few words of greetings with a man named Jitendra, who he'd worked with at a construction site until a few months ago. When Amit had last seen him, he wore only a threadbare pair of shorts and sandals. Seeing his comfortable kurta-pyjama set made Amit swallow hard.

'Pickers in the local community are essential for our business model,' Rahul said. 'They bring us hard-to-reach plastics, and they do a lot of sorting to ensure plastics end up with the right enzymes to break them down. We employ them directly and encourage them to join a collective so their voices are always heard – and we hope to transform the economy in the local community in the next decade.'

They followed the sorted plastic fragments along chutes to more huge vats, where the enzymes broke them down. Before they entered these rooms, Rahul asked Amit to wear a mask and a hazard suit.

Amit narrowed his eyes at the protective gear. 'Why do we need these if there is no burning?'

'Some plastic monomers are toxic for humans. None should escape into the atmosphere, but we take these precautions until we can stabilise them again.'

Next, Rahul showed Amit an example of the outcome. 'This is virgin PET, a type of plastic,' he said as they approached a large barrel filled to the rim with whitish crystals. He lifted some in his hands and encouraged Amit to do the same. Amit realised they were transparent, and they sat in his hand with hardly any weight.

'We sell plastic in this raw state to companies who then use it to produce fresh items. Consumers buy these, everything from shopping bags to clothing to food containers, use them, and then return them to us, and the process repeats. A circular system where no plastic is ever wasted.'

Amit shifted his hand to allow the stream of plastic to trickle back into the barrel, so different from the black ash that Priyanka had once swept from the street outside their home every day. Clenching his fist, Amit turned away from Rahul, his shoulders shaking.

Lakshan, light of his life, had loved to play around in the heaped ash piles and often came home covered from head to toe in soot like an Aghori. Born two years after they arrived in Muzaffarnagar, he was so small when he came into the world, such a tiny mite. In those four short years, he grew into a thin wisp of a boy with a huge, crooked smile and a curiosity for everything. But a cough plagued him, far worse than Amit's, and sometimes he could do nothing more than sit on the bed he shared with his sister, spluttering and rasping, battling for each breath. When he hacked up blood in his fourth year, Amit grew desperate. He carried Lakshan to a health clinic, but Lakshan breathed his last breath during the examination.

The doctor at the clinic told Amit there was nothing he could have done. 'Respiratory failure,' he said. 'Likely caused by toxins in the air.' He explained more about the low air quality in and around Muzaffarnagar, and the various contributing factors, including the illegal burning of plastics in the paper and sugar mills, and Amit gaped at him, realising how his ignorant labour had contributed to his son's premature death.

When he turned away from Rahul, Amit glimpsed his outline in the stainless-steel surfaces around him. The blurry figure transformed into the man his son would never become, the man who would never step foot in this magical place which would prevent future plastic burning. If only it had opened a decade earlier.

He buried his head in his arm, the familiar tickling in his throat almost a relief now. When the cough erupted from his chest, it masked the bitter tears that streaked his cheeks.

~~~

Returning home that evening to the usual competing aromas of fresh sizzling spices and pungent wood smoke, Amit told Priyanka to bring Diya from the other room.

Arms folded, Diya refused to meet his eye. 'Is it done, then?' 'Beti, you like working there, yes?'

She lifted her head, eyes widening, and nodded forcefully. 'Yes, Paapaa, very much.'

'They say you do good work, that it would be a shame to lose you. That your English is really coming along.' He held out his hands. 'I am not so stubborn that I cannot admit when I am wrong. But I know that your education is important, which is why I suggest a compromise.'

He relayed to her what Dr Uppal had told him, about how she wouldn't progress from a sales team assistant without a formal education, but that there would be no problem with her working part-time while she completed her studies.

'So, if you put your wages into paying for your education and study hard,' he continued, 'I see no reason to stop you.'

'Oh, Paapaa!' She threw herself into his arms.

'Besides,' he said, 'I will be nearby to ensure this recycling plant really is everything it says it is. I've accepted a job there, too.'

While Priyanka laid out their food that evening, Amit slipped into the bedroom. When he emerged, smiling, to share the meal with his wife and daughter, he settled on a mat in his new maroon kurta.

Coby

by Laura Baggaley

"**G**et off our land!"

Her grandmother's voice leaps from her mouth, surprising her almost as much as it startles the stranger.

"W-what?"

Lisa is about to repeat herself – *this is our land, you're trespassing!* – but then she remembers and the words evaporate.

"What?" the man says again.

Her mind rushes. All the emotions and upheaval of the past weeks form a torrent of images in her head, and she can't find words for any of them. The *For Sale* sign. Grandad's quiet sadness. Grandma's belligerent pretending. Lisa's parents, sorting and packing and asking the same questions again and again, '*Do you want to keep this? And this? Shall we get rid of this?*' Even the farmhouse feels shrunken by the sudden disturbance.

It had never occurred to Lisa that the farm wouldn't be theirs forever.

The trespasser is staring at her, crouched between the trees, eyes big in his pale face. He reminds her of a squirrel, paused in the eye of danger, ready to run. Lisa feels a surge of fury and jumps from the stile into the dew-damp grass.

"This is private property!" she says, striding across the orchard towards him.

"Oh! I'm sorry – I'm so sorry. I didn't – didn't mean to . . ."

He fumbles with objects on the ground, clumsy with hurry. Drawing nearer, Lisa sees what he's trying to pack away. A large hard-cover case lies open on the ground; arranged neatly in the lid are rows of small glass containers, assorted metal scoops, a notebook covered in black scribbles, a computer tablet, and various unidentifiable tools that look like they might be for measuring. Her mind leaps to an explanation.

"Sorry, sorry, sorry," mutters the stranger, crouching as he slots glass tubes into a foam holder.

"Are you a spy?"

He stops and stares up at her, a look of pure confusion on his face. Lisa realises that he's younger than she thought – mid-twenties, perhaps, only a bit older than her eldest brother.

"You know, an agricultural spy! Testing our soil fertility without permission!"

Another possibility occurs to her and her face shines red with embarrassment.

"Oh!" She speaks more quietly. "Do you work for the company? The new owners?"

His expression is a shifting mix of perplexity and shame. Keeping his eyes on her, he straightens up, opening his hands in a gesture of innocence.

"No. Not a spy, not part of a company. I don't know anything about any of that. I'm sorry, you're right. I shouldn't be here without permission. I had a hunch, see. I was excited to test it, so I snuck in. Just to take a few samples, you wouldn't even know I'd been . . ."

Standing up, he is taller than Lisa. His trousers are a little short for his lanky frame and he wears a scruffy jumper that seems out of keeping with his sophisticated-looking equipment. Wrong-footed by his apology, she folds her arms, glaring.

"What kind of samples? What d'you mean? What is all this stuff?"

"I'm prospecting." He smiles, and Lisa's glare dissolves.

"For *gold*?!"

The smile turns into a laugh. It tinges his cheeks pink, transforming him from terrified owl to amused chipmunk.

"For microbes."

"Huh." Lisa has no idea what he's talking about. She doesn't know whether this is a thing she's supposed to know, whether she should be embarrassed by her ignorance or not, so she resumes and intensifies her glare.

"Microscopic organisms," he elaborates. "In the soil. So yeah, it is to do with soil fertility, sort of."

"Huh." Lisa doesn't know what question will get the answers she needs. "Why?"

"You see the apple trees over there?"

"Quick Adder Corner? Yeah."

"Is that what you call it?"

Lisa feels a pang. She and her brothers have named every part of her grandparents' farm. A vivid memory of a rainy afternoon springs into her head, felt-tip pens at the kitchen table, earnestly drawing all the elements onto tea-stained maps: the spreading oak tree (The Ship), the pond (The Treacherous Mire), the big willow (HQ), the compost heap (Worm Palace). . .

". . . and you see, I noticed those trees are much healthier than the ones in – in Adder Corner?"

His nearly accurate use of the family language snaps her back to the present. Because it's true: one area of the orchard has always produced better apples, apples that are sweeter and more copious than anywhere else on the farm.

"So I started investigating the other side of that hedge –"

"That's not our land."

"I know. It was a dumping ground. More than twenty-five years ago."She gives him a suspicious look; he can't be old enough to remember. "How do you know that?"

"I was digging. Metaphorical – paper digging!" He glances at her, hoping for a laugh, a concession, then quickly carries on. "I've been doing research in the local archives."

He sounds weirdly excited and she has no idea what he's going on about.

"What for?"

"I discovered that, back in the 1990s, the landowner let loads of junk pile up in that bit of the field – old machinery, tools, oil cans, plastic containers. It was festering, toxic. A guy called Brian Gibson –"

"That's my grandfather!"

"Oh, that makes sense. Well, your grandfather took his neighbours to court, made them clean it up, on the basis that it was affecting his land. I found the papers, and Brian claimed that –"

It felt strange hearing him say Grandad's name, and Lisa was still confused.

"But why were you looking?"

"Because I want to know why that bit of orchard seems happier than those trees. Because it might be to do with a pollution legacy. And it might, just might, lead me to discover a new strain of bacteria that's helping the soil recover."

"Oh. I see. I think."

She turns over what he's said, wondering what to make of it. Rubs her eyes and discovers crumbs of sleepy dust; she hasn't washed her face or cleaned her teeth yet today. He is looking at her intently and she feels suddenly embarrassed. Her t-shirt is ancient, the fabric thin from a thousand washes, and she's wearing yesterday's grubby shorts.

"So, uh –" she tries to get things clear in her head, "It would help farming. If you discover something new?"

He nods, with little fast movements like a wind-up toy.

"Yes! Yes exactly!" He takes a breath, then gabbles, "Did you know that in one square metre of soil there could be half a million microbes? The whole of life depends on them. Literally. Life on earth. When you look through a microscope – it's, it's amazing! Half a teaspoon of soil contains a whole universe. Hundreds of the tiniest creatures, different species, working together without even realising it, spontaneously creating intricate biological architectures. It's phenomenal!"

"Oh."

"And we're discovering microbes that can eat plastic, that can clear oil spills! I mean, humans are causing so many problems for the natural world, but the solutions might be all around us. If we just look closer."

There's a silence between them. He seems to be waiting for her to pass a verdict. A tiny breeze rustles the branches overhead, as if trying to hurry Lisa along. She struggles to work out what to say; her brain feels stuffed with thoughts, as congested as a nose with a cold. Perhaps sensing this, he speaks into the pause.

"If I can take these samples back to the lab, run some tests, check whether there's anything worth investigating, then it would just be a case of maybe coming back in a few weeks' time? Following up if –"

"You're too late!" She interrupts, rising anger and sadness making her voice suddenly loud and aggressive. "The farm's being sold."

The perturbed look on his face infuriates her. She keeps talking, irrationally trying to divert her pain onto him.

"A massive agribusiness is gonna be taking over in a few weeks! As soon as the contract's signed, they'll be rolling through here, ripping up these trees, demolishing the hedgerows . . ."

"No! That's –"

His horrified exclamation makes her even angrier.

"That's what? That's shit? Damn right it is!"

Tears sting her eyes and she realises she can't hold them back.

"Wait!"

He calls after her but she's already at the stile, up and over and running as fast as she can, trying to outrun reality.

Much later in the day, when the farmhouse is full of bustle and the sun is high overhead, Lisa returns to the orchard. The microbe man has gone; as he promised, there's nothing to show he was ever there. Lisa walks very slowly around every tree, lightly touching the bark here and there, tilting her head back sometimes to look up into the leafy branches overhead. Each tree is its own world, inhabited by multitudes – insects, lichen, beetles, ants, birds, squirrels. She remembers what the stranger said: apparently millions of microbes live under and around the trees too. Invisible galaxies of life, making all living existence possible.

The orchard has been Lisa's favourite place for so long, it's impossible to believe it will be destroyed. She's already cried for an hour today. Now she takes deep breaths and tries to memorise every bit of it.

The final trip to the farm feels like a funeral.

Months have passed. More visits, more packing boxes and tears. The sale has been delayed, and the pause is poisonous. Emotions have swelled to fill the gap, growing and intensifying. Lisa's parents have become even louder in their self-justification, gripped with irremediable guilt.

"I'm not a farmer!"

"You could be." Grandma doesn't let her son off easily.

"I never wanted to be a farmer! I'm a geek, I'm good at maths. Accountancy is my thing, and you've just never got that."

"Your children might want to take on the farm. It's a family legacy."

"Now come on," Lisa's mother intervenes, "That's not fair! We can't give up our lives to run a farm just in case one of our offspring might happen to want it a decade from now. We live in the city. We are an urban family."

"Lisa loves the farm."

"We all love the farm!"

"Lisa is a born farmer."

"She's sixteen!"

Grandma vents feelings through arguing. Grandad is silent, mournful as a lame dog, grieving the truth that they 'can't manage' on their own any more. Lisa tries to block it all out; perhaps if she pretends it isn't happening the sale will never go through.

On the last day, no-one bickers. Mum, Dad, Lisa and her two brothers drive up to the farmhouse and get out of the car in silence. The curtains are gone from the windows; the building looks depressed. Grandad and Grandma are standing in the empty kitchen. They seem lost, but manage to smile when the family troop in.

"They'll be here in an hour," says Grandad, "Why don't you kids have a last look round?"

Lisa feels disconnected, as if her heart has been shut in a box to protect it from all the sadness. Her brothers chat as they go, treating the day as normal whatever they might be feeling. The hour passes – disappears – so quickly that Lisa feels cheated. In a moment, it seems, they are back on the driveway, watching the unfamiliar car crunch over the gravel.

A man in a shiny grey suit approaches and starts shaking the adults' hands.

Lisa is distracted by a lanky figure who stands near the distant gate, half-hidden behind a tree just beyond the farm boundary.

The suited agent invites the family indoors, leading them into the farmhouse as if he owns it. Ignoring them, Lisa sprints down the drive.

"Lisa?" Mum calls after her, "Where are you going?"

"I'll be there in a minute!" Lisa shouts back, shooing her away.

Lisa's brain is bursting with questions but when she reaches the stranger all the words have suddenly gone. They stare at each other for a second.

"I'm not on your land this time," he says, with a half smile.

"What are you doing here?" She's breathless.

"I knew today was the handover," the microbe man says. "Hoped I'd see you."

"You're the buyer?"

"I wish!"

Her tiny hope fizzles and she wonders why he's smiling.

"But I *did* discover something new." In his delight, he sounds like a child revealing a playground secret.

"From prospecting?"

"Yes!"

"And . . . ?"

"And it's a previously undiscovered strain of bacteria that could be of international significance in the context of pollution-management and soil-improvement." He sounds like he's reciting an official document and confirms it with a confession: "That's from the press release."

She feels a flare of irritation. What does it matter, when today they lose the farm?

"Have you just come here to show off?"

"No! Listen! When we realised what I'd found in your orchard, the lab went into overdrive. Lodged an appeal for an ecological survey. Delayed things."

Lisa is wary. "So?"

"Then my bosses started applying for research grants, conservation funds, science endowments, talking to universities and charities, trying to get private sponsorship – basically doing everything they could to raise the money to buy the farm instead of the agribusiness."

"My family never said."

"They wouldn't know. Estate agents are cagey as hell, they always keep people in the dark."

"So who has bought it?"

"It's a consortium. A group of like-minded organisations. Concerned with microbial research, sustainable agriculture, heritage farming. We've all had to cooperate, make space for each other's obsessions!"

Lisa's heart accelerates as if she's on the start line of a race.

"So what will happen to the farm?"

"It's becoming a collaborative research centre. In partnership with the lab where I work up the road."

Her heartbeat bolts ahead of her brain.

"So . . . the orchard . . . "

"No demolition! The farm is safe!"

Lisa is frozen in a moment of disbelief. Can it be true? She stares at him, uncertain. His face is open, smiling its chipmunk smile, and she begins to believe. She can hardly breathe for joy. The farm is safe.

"Come on," Lisa can't wait to share the news, "Let's go inside and tell them."

They run towards the farmhouse, feet flying. At the threshold, Lisa pauses for a second.

"One question," she asks.

"Uh-huh?"

"What's your name?"

"Um, really it's William. But everyone calls me Coby."

"Coby?"

"'Cause of the microbes."

Lisa laughs and pushes open the door.

Microbes at the Ready

by Beatrice Smyth

A t the annual convention of Farm Animals and Associated Creatures Together (FAACT), there was consternation. This was not the first year of such disquiet, but it had reached a new level. The trout spoke first about the horrors of living in the river beside the farm, with slurry gushing into his home after heavy rainfall. He told frankly of the lack of food and oxygen, and with great sadness he remembered family and friends lost to the pollution. The moorhen took the floor next and echoed the challenges of what she called swimming in a cow's rear end, the horrible slime in the river and the awful stench. It was impossible to keep her feathers clean, and that was the least of it. She trembled when telling of her fears for the health of her young. Then the swan got involved and things got heated.

With the authority that comes with being a special creature, the swan did not hold back, accusing the cows of being heartless killers. The cows were shocked, as they had never realised how much damage their daily lives were causing. They couldn't understand how the humdrum of chewing the cud and lining up at the milking parlour could be so dangerous, and, as herbivores, they strongly objected to being called killers. One cow was particularly incensed and bawled at the swan, accusing him of lying, but the swan was having none of it. He raised his wings and hissed fiercely. They were about to come to blows when the heron spoke.

Until now the heron had been observing quietly. She was good at watching and contemplating. She had also been places, to other farms and beyond, and had seen what could be done with a bit of will and imagination. That, though, she had to admit, might be the difficult part. It's tricky to change one's ways, she thought to herself, but with a deep breath, she figured it was worth a go. "Are the microbes here?" the heron asked. "Huh?" and "The what?" said a lot of blank faces.

The microbes had long been excluded from the annual convention, but years of lobbying and advocacy had finally ended the discrimination. They were permitted to join for the first time this year, although so far they had been silent. A lifetime of being sidelined and misunderstood left them reluctant to put their heads above the parapet. Microbes, or microscopic organisms as they are more formally known, had a bad name on the farm. They were used to getting dirty looks, being called filthy germs, and shouldering the blame for every illness and calamity. They were also petrified of the swan, who strongly objected to their presence at the convention, and who now turned his anger on the heron. "What would they know anyway?" bellowed the swan. "They're not even animals. And they're the cause of the problem. It's the blasted microbes and the stinky algae that are clogging up the river in the first place."

Thankfully, the heron had depths of patience and was good at bringing calm to turmoil. After reminding the swan to renew his diversity training, the heron painted a picture of what life could be like, with clean water and sweet-smelling air. That got the attention of the crowd, even if they didn't quite believe such a change was possible. The heron was very knowledgeable and explained that unruly out-of-control microbes, like those causing damage to the river, were different to a properly engineered microbial system. The microbes themselves aren't the problem, she told the audience. If we feed them lots of slurry out in the open air, then of course they're going to run amok in the river; it'd be like the sheepdog stealing the farmer's doughnuts, gorging herself and then feeling queasy. The sheepdog would never do such a thing, but it lightened the mood and got a giggle from the crowd.

Back to the matter in hand, the heron described how providing microbes with a regular well-balanced diet and a proper home could transform everyone's lives on the farm. Instead of going straight on to the fields, the cattle slurry could be put into a sealed oxygen-free tank called an anaerobic digester, which is a comfortable, heated environment for the microbes to thrive. There, our friends the microbes would work hard to produce methane for renewable energy, along with a less polluting fertiliser in the form of digestate.

The microbes stood proud, and the crowd started to get excited. But the prize bull thought it was time for a reality check. He had also visited other farms; he was educated, and he knew his stuff. "All good in theory," he interjected, "but it's not that easy in practice. What you're talking about is a circular economy. Yes, it's based on the microbes, who are willing and able, but for it to function effectively we need integrated policies across the nexus of agriculture, energy and environment. We require cohesive thinking to link the food, fuel and water sectors, as well as planning permits, grid connections and a suitable incentive scheme." The barn owl started to snore. The chickens looked confused. The farmyard cat twitched his whiskers in distaste. He found big words awfully boring. The prize bull was right, but he was losing the crowd. Fortunately, his buddy the sheepdog was on hand.

The sheepdog was a canine of action. She was quickwitted and a master of organisation. "Right," said the sheepdog, "leave it with me. I'll chat to the farmer, and I'll iron out the details with the council, the engineers, and the environment agency. If there are any issues, I have a direct line to the minister. With everyone on board, it shouldn't take long to get it sorted. Once the bigwigs have signed it off, I'll round up the builders and get them to step on it. Microbes at the ready. Your time has come."

There were cheers and there were hugs. And, more importantly, there was a new determination from the farm animals and creatures to work together for a cleaner future.

The Greener Tyne

by Matt Edmundson

T he boat kept station at the mouth of the Tyne. Ahead a large
coaster was just passing the twin Shields piers on its way upriver. Eric could make out the name *Sunflower* painted in gold letters
on the stern. He'd seen the ship a lot recently on his trips to and from
Tyneside, there was an important bioremediation project happening
down in Cornwall and this ship was part of those efforts.

Centuries of tin and copper mining had brought wealth to a few
and hard, dangerous work to many, and had also generated huge
amounts of arsenic as a byproduct. This had contaminated the soil
around the old workings, useless land filled with deadly poison. But
something had shifted in the way the economy regarded the situation;
that soil wasn't filled with poison; it was a rich resource to be brought
back into use (although it was very much still a deadly poison if not
handled correctly).

Arsenic-resistant plants could be grown on the spoil heaps, slowly
enriching themselves on the discarded metals. These plants could then
be harvested, and brought to the biofactories of the Tyne, where they

were ground down and fed to communities of engineered bacteria. These specialists could recover the copper and tin missed by the first miners, taking the raw atoms and performing their biochemical magic to turn them into potent antimicrobials, or as additives for complex alloys; even the arsenic could find a use in a new generation of micro-electronics, or in anti-cancer drugs. The plants themselves were both food for the bacteria and also a resource in themselves; other modified microorganisms could convert the plant mass into pharmaceuticals, or bioplastics, or perfume scents; any complex organic molecule was potentially within reach. As Eric waited his turn to enter the river, he saw a tanker heading out into the North Sea, carrying biofuels.

A happy little chime sounded from the navigation computer. Eric approved the request from the Tyne pilot and gave over control of his boat to the automated system. He furled the photovoltaic sails and locked down the tubular wind turbine in the centre of the deck and switched to battery power; the river was busy, and he didn't want to be blown into the path of another vessel. He looked down from the bridge, across the deck of the ship, as it made its way along the river. Only a few dozen metres long with a three-story deckhouse on the stern shaped like an old-style Chinese junk and carrying a cargo of waste plastic, sorted by type in its three little holds; one for PET, one for polystyrene and one of mixed, scooped straight out of the sea and not smelling particularly appealing. The rotting seaweed would at least earn him a small bonus as biomass though. The deckhouse consisted of the bridge on the highest level with two decks of living quarters below.

Beneath the level of the main deck were the gubbins of the ship; the batteries and engines, fresh and waste water tanks, the processors for the automated systems. He made his way downstairs from the bridge into the kitchen. Freya was sitting at the kitchen table, working on her tablet. She was scanning through the global commodity index; information constantly updating, showing what needed picking up where and to where it needed taking, so whatever the route you had planned there was always cargo to take on somewhere along it.

"Once we've dropped off this lot there's a pickup from the waste-water plant," she said.

"Oh. You sure there's nothing else on there?" asked Eric as he put the kettle on.

"Afraid not. Besides, we need to empty the ship's wastewater tanks soon anyway, it'd be nice to get paid for it instead of paying to get rid of it."

"Ugh, fine, book it in. Fancy a tea?"

"No, I'm good, thanks."

Eric poured tea into his mug and snuck a biscuit out of the tin.

"Right, I'm off back upstairs, check our progress."

As he entered the bridge, he saw they were just passing the *Sunflower*, moored up beside a biofactory. The crew had already started unloading. The smell of flowers and cut grass reached him as he sipped his tea. He saw flashes of yellow and black; the ship was aptly named. The oils in the sunflower seeds would make a good feedstock for the microbes.

Eric continued watching the activity of the river and its banks, vessels loading and unloading, smaller boats picking their way around their larger siblings. Eventually the Ouseburn came into sight. Two figures were trying to manoeuvre a large thick square of stiff fabric onto a cargo bike. "I wonder if that's mushroom leather?" he thought as he passed by. He knew the Victoria tunnel ran under the city of Newcastle, once connecting the quayside to the colliery; after the colliery was closed the tunnels were largely abandoned. In the 1920s they'd tried converting the tunnel into a mushroom farm with little success. It took over a century before bespoke engineered fungi were developed that could be processed into sustainable leather with the same texture and properties of the original material, finally allowing a mycological garden to flourish beneath the city.

Finally, their boat arrived at the Dunston Staithes; the tall wooden jetty where coal from pits on the south side of the Tyne were loaded onto the ships. Today there was a market being held on them, and Eric could see the crowded stalls as he tied up the boat. He climbed up to the staithes and sought out Tony, the market organiser.

"Hello Tony! You got something for me?"

"Aye, we've stacked up all the packaging in the usual place. We've had a couple of fishmongers up from North Shields so some of the polystyrene stinks of fish, but it should still be good."

"Cheers Tones, I'll get it loaded up."

The two men began transferring armfuls of plastic packaging onto the boat, the light but bulky polystyrene being a particular hassle. Once they'd finished, they made their farewells and Eric cast off to make the short hop further upriver to Blaydon. He approached the dock at one of the biofactories and saw a figure making their way down the quayside, waving cheerily. As he got closer he saw it was Flora, the dock manager, and waved back in response.

"Hiya hinny, what have you got for me this time?" she asked.

"PET in hold one, polystyrene in two and mixed in three, plus a stack of mixed on deck from the market."

"Ah, if I'd known you'd be stopping off there I'd have asked you to pick me up a couple of stotties. Never mind! We'll get this unloaded for you. If you pop into the office Sally'll sort out your payment."

Eric thanked her and made his way towards the main building as the deck crew began offloading the cargo. Opening the door, he was hit by the smell of a dozen different spices; he enjoyed visiting the factory, it always reminded him of Christmas. The receptionist buzzed him through into the main office and he made his way to Sally's desk.

"Hiya Eric! How're things?" They chatted for a while, catching up whilst the shipment was unloaded.

"This place always smells amazing," said Eric. "I've got no idea how you take plastic that stinks of fish and turn it into something that smells so good."

"Why don't I give you a quick tour? I can't believe I've not shown you round before!"

"That sounds great!"

They made their way onto the factory floor. Huge cylindrical vats stood in rows, floor to ceiling. Pipes in profusion ran around the space, seemingly connecting everything to everything else, disappearing into walls, under the floors and out of the roof. The smell of spice was even stronger in here, intense and only a notch under being overwhelming. Benches were dotted around here and there, bearing pieces of equipment. At a few of these stations people busied themselves with testing samples and analysing data.

"This is where the magic happens!" said Sally. "We've got a water-mill down by the river where we grind up the plastic; it needs to be in tiny bits before we can feed it to our bacteria in here." She patted one of the giant cylinders. "In this bioreactor we say auf wiedersehen PET and hello vanilla!"

"So, you go from PET plastic to something you can put in ice cream? Won't you get microplastics into my desert?"

"No, that's the beauty of chemistry. PET is made up of the same molecule repeated loads of times and joined up in a long chain, a polymer. That molecule is very close to being the molecule called vanillin, which gives you the taste and smell of vanilla. We've designed our bacteria to be able to take the PET molecule, break some of the chemical bonds and form new ones so the molecule is now vanillin. No plastic, all vanilla!" "Ah, so I'm not eating plastic?"

"No. Hmm, I guess it's like if you had a caterpillar, and it turned into a butterfly. If you ate the butterfly, you wouldn't be eating the caterpillar. Although I'd suggest not eating either…"

Eric chuckled. "I think you need a better metaphor than caterpillar ice cream."

"Ha, no! How about it being like if you fertilise a field of crops? You spread manure onto the field and the plants take up the nutrients from that and turn it into fruit or vegetables? You're eating the same molecules that made up the manure, but the plants have turned them into apples or potatoes."

"That sounds more palatable. Agh, you've just reminded me we've got to do a pickup of "fertiliser" at the sewerage plant later. Not looking forward to that!"

"Don't poo-poo the poo! It's an amazing resource, very rich in nutrients. If you process it correctly, you can make a great feedstock from it. Back in the old days people used to really value it. They'd pay good money to get it and spread it on their crops. Somewhere along the way we lost sight of just how much value it had and started dumping it into the rivers and seas. Literally flushing money away…"

"Well, I'll be sure to remember that if one of the cargo seals breaks and I'm sailing around in a floating toilet…"

Sally laughed. "Hopefully it won't be as bad as that!"

They continued their tour. They passed the bioreactors for cinnamon and limonene, and on to the bespoke pharmaceuticals.

"We have a library of engineered bacteria. Depending on which flavouring or drug is needed we can load up the reactor with a few cells of the strain we want. The molecules that make up plastic are a great starting point for so many things!"

They finished their tour and made their way back to the office.

"Thanks Sally, that was really interesting! It's good to see what actually happens to the plastic I'm carrying around."

"Glad you enjoyed it!"

Bidding Sally farewell, Eric made his way back to his boat. Freya was on deck, helping the dock team unload the last of the cargo. As he climbed aboard, she was just closing the final hatch on the empty hold.

"All sorted?" she asked.

"Yep, all done. Suppose we'd better get that sewerage loaded now..."

"I suppose so!" she chuckled.

They stood on the bridge as the boat headed back down river, through the centre of Newcastle, picking their way through the busy river traffic and passing the new biofactories on either bank.

"It's good to see the river busy again. It helped drive a whole industrial revolution," mused Eric.

"Yes... and helped cause a lot of pollution problems we're still dealing with."

"Ha, that's true too. At least now we're not just digging up resources to make things just to throw them away."

"Yep, the river sends stuff out, it gets used, then it all comes flowing back up to get turned into something new again. And with us carting it all over the place in between. Speaking of which, you'd best get back up to the bridge and make sure we're still on course."

They continued down the Tyne, flowing into the North Sea and out into the world.

I'll Tell You, Shall I, Something I Remember?

by Alexandra Burkitt

I remember the day when the trees fell silent.

The taste of their sugars had been with me for my whole life. I knew them from the moment I germinated from my mother's spore and joined my siblings in our great underground web.

The trees let us into their roots, and our network joined with their network to form a great city underground. We felt the passage of time in the trees' rhythms: the pulse of sugar for spring, the long slow sleep of winter. Their roots sang with chemical signals which spoke of day and night, leaves growing and branches falling, caterpillars grazing and birds hatching. They tied us together to other families like ours, other networks of silent fungi underground. And we in turn joined them to other trees, passing the flavour of chemicals from one to another like calling, like song. We grew out into the soil, sisters and daughters and cousins, and searched for the nutrients that we needed, and then we shared them with the trees.

Our world may be dark, but it was never empty. The soil is full of other fungi, in their own networks or growing alone, cousins all. Some are like us, greeting the trees, joining with their roots. Others prey upon the trees or feed up the fallen leaves. There are stranger things too, much less like us. Single cells, wandering or still, all have their own chemical songs for us to taste. The bacteria which live on our surfaces, on the trees, in the soil itself, send their calls out into the soil and water. The soil sings with chemicals, and all of them tell their stories for those of us who know how to understand them.

Occasionally, larger things send out their messages into the soil. Things like the huge earth movers, the worms which brush past our threads, or centipedes many legged hunting for the springtails and mites that hunt me and my fungi-cousins in turn. Sometimes, rarely, we taste things larger still, strange and other and impossibly vast. They leave tunnels, huge empty spaces in our webs of siblings that we have to grow around. There may be distant vibrations as the earth moves, odd threads of fur and the distant taste of musk. If, above the ground, there are things larger still, we do not know. They do not come into our soil.

The first sign of something wrong was a strange taste from the trees. It was different from anything we had met before, alien and new. The winter was over; the trees should have spoken of growing and new leaves and spring arriving, but instead they tasted of stress and sleep and wrong. The leaves fell unseasonably upon the soil until the worms brought them down to us and our cousins turned them back into earth. Still the trees sang of their hurting, and of a disease never met before. They became quieter. There was little sugar, then less, then one day none.

My siblings, joined with my cell and my mother's, lost the taste of the trees when I did. We hoped that they would wake again, and that perhaps this out of season winter would turn back to spring with time. Some of us slept. But the height of summer came, and the trees were still silent.

We had been used to vibrations in the soil from the digging creatures, but what came next was larger and stranger and far more frightening. The ground shook, and the water smelt of petrol, and then the trees were gone. Not just silent, as they had been before, but vanished entirely. Their roots were torn away from us. Sisters were broken, their cells fractured as the trees were dug from the ground, their strands broken as the small roots snapped. All that remained were empty spaces left behind, where we had no one to sense and send back the tastes of the soil to the web. We did not know what had taken our trees. We only knew they had disappeared. The alien taste that had heralded their loss was all that remained.

When the trees had gone, the rest of the soil dwellers fell silent. With no fallen leaves, there was nothing for our cousins to eat. Some cousins, those that could, sent out missions to the surface, sent spores up into the air to find new trees. We had no way of knowing if they succeeded. If they landed in good soil again, it would be too far away for our web to reach and to carry the news back to us. The worms moved away, and the other great earth movers followed. Even the ghostly giants no longer carved their burrows through the soil. I grew outwards, sent strands further from the centre of our web in the search for new trees. I found some, with time, but they were strange things. They did not taste like our old trees had before the sickness came. I reached out to their roots, but they did not let me inside.

The cold had come two times over when change came again. In days, between what would have been breaths of the trees had our trees still been there, holes appeared in our network once more. The soil was moved from above by strange hands that smelt of metal rather than of fur. When we grew back into the new spaces, we found cells there of a type that we had never seen before, and they brought a new flavour with them. It was a strange taste, like cold and light and not-soil; it did not taste of the forest. At first, it reminded us of the alien things that had made the trees fall silent, and we were afraid. But the new cells sat amongst us and the other soil dwellers, and they found a place in the tapestry of underground life.

They grew, and spread, and moved between us. Slowly, the taste of the disease which had stolen our trees began to fade, until it was so faint that we didn't notice it was gone for good.

Spring came with the warming soil, and new plants sent down their roots. But something was different. The message came back through the network. A root song which we had not heard for many seasons. Trees like our old ones, but without the alien taste. The seeds had lain in the soil, and now, free from the illness, they were germinating again.

They let us into their roots, and we sent them food, and they grew. And through it all, the strange new cells kept the taste of disease away.

I remember when the trees went silent. I remember when the new trees spoke.

Cake and Compost

by Sharon Godiff

"Boys, boys. Eat your breakfast, hurry up, we're going to be late."

I quickly assemble cream cheese sandwiches and fill their lunch boxes with the last two cartons of juice, and in desperation for a sweet treat I peel and share a dry satsuma and a handful of coco pops and divide between two snack bags.

"Coco Pops for afters?" enquires Charlie.

"Yes" I smile. "All your friends would have them if they could."

Satisfied with my explanation he continues eating the remains of his breakfast Coco Pops. Good job, they like them, and they are fortified with vitamins, I think smirking. The barking of the dog heralds the clack of the letter box, which fills me with dread. Bills and final demands, sickness and worry arrive through the door daily. Scanning the handful of envelopes, I decide they can all wait till later, as the boys are tearing around still not dressed. When eventually we're all ready and about to leave, an evil stench emanates from the rear end of my little

Princess and it cannot be ignored. I sigh knowing I'll have to change her, and we'll be late again.

Walking back, Tula trots obediently beside me, the lead attached to the handle of the buggy. Grace, clean and fragrant for the time being, is anything but graceful as her name suggests, as she sprawls dangling her legs over either side and I can see her favourite smiling frog wellies bobbing. I push her along deep in thought. Charlie's teacher had pulled me to one side when I dropped them off. Smiling kindly "is everything alright" she enquired. Then, still smiling but in a concerned tone, she told me Charlie's having difficulty concentrating in class; and as she'd noticed that recently we're frequently late, she wondered if there was anything wrong. She was right of course, but after another poor night's sleep I wanted to scream: "Actually, Miss Pilling, my husband walked out 2 weeks ago! He's spending money from our account like water, and I don't have enough food in the cupboards to feed the three kids never mind the dog, and the mortgage is due next week."

I didn't of course. I thanked her for bringing it to my attention, said I'd have a chat with him after school and I'd let her know. Well, at least Sam seems okay? He ran into school with his best friend Jessica.

Just then, the autumn sun makes a rare appearance and, although significantly diluted, its warm glow on my chilled cheeks has strength enough to darken the reactive lenses in my glasses. Then Grace starts singing and my mood elevates. So, I take her and Tula across to the park, and watch their joy as they run and play in the crisp golden leaves that lie on the ground, her squeals of glee encouraging Tula to yap and jump excitedly, which makes Grace giggle and squeal more. A simple pleasure for us all, which is a blessing. I sit on a bench in the bright sunshine, smiling at my happy child and little dog. I have hope. Not that he will return to me and his children, because this time I wouldn't have him back. This time is different. This time I'm not pregnant, weak, or stupid, believing his lies. This time I'm angry. My hope is that we will be okay and much happier without him. Because this time he's not having his fun then worming his way back into our lives.

I let her play a little longer whilst I reread an email. Yesterday I'd cried when I'd received notification that we'd got to the top of the list for an allotment. Believing I couldn't manage that and everything else alone. But I do manage. Each time he disappears for days or weeks I manage. And being a responsible semi-self-sufficient family and getting the kids involved had been my dream. Pete was never part of that, it was my idea to ensure the kids were environmentally aware. Feeling uplifted and determined, I get up off the bench and join in with the fun, throwing the leaves high in the air. Then to my surprise one of the brown leaves is rectangular and plastic and it flutters into my hand and turns out to be a tenner, and it is my turn to squeal with delight at my literal windfall.

Back home I put the £10 safe under the clock. Searching through the meagre contents of the fridge-freezer and cupboards, I conjure up another substantial meal. I've become an expert and soon the ripe veg drawer and a can of baked beans are blended, creating a tasty, thick warming soup for lunch; and there will be plenty for the hungry boys when they get home too, supplemented with cheese toasties. Whilst stirring the pan, I smile in anticipation, imagining the fragrant bunches of fresh vegetables and herbs I'll be harvesting from our own allotment.

Grace, with her tummy full, naps with Tula snuggled beside her. I tidy up, then make coffee and sit in the comfy chair next to the oven, which is warming up as I intend to make scones for after tea and for their lunch boxes. I pick up the pile of letters, trying to decide which ones will upset me least. I ignore the brown envelopes, they're always bad news, and open a white one. It's the bank statement! I feel sick, as the balance is well into the overdraft. In desperation but still strong, I ring Pete: his phone is switched off. I compose another text.

"Pete what the hell is going on! I don't care who you're with this time. But I have no money to feed the kids, pay bills or put petrol in the car, and what about the mortgage?"

Surprisingly later that night, I get a reply.

"I need to sort stuff. You've got it all wrong, you know I love you. I just need some space. If you're desperate ask your parents for help. Tell the kids I love them." Incensed, I called his number, he'd turned it off again. The coward!

Later that week, I'm relieved to find money has been paid into the account, and the mortgage is paid. Not having that debt is a huge weight off my shoulders.

Another week has passed and it's half term. As I can now afford the petrol, the kids are off to my parents' house at the seaside.

"It's been ages since we've stayed with Nana and Grandad" says Sam who's 5, whilst packing his stuff into his beloved Thomas the Tank bag. "Grandad always plays football with me."

Charlie, who at 8 has chosen his camouflaged backpack, says teasingly, "I hope Nana makes a big chocolate cake, just for me, because I'm her favourite."

Sam falls for it and whines, "I want chocolate cake; she likes me and Gracie too." Grace is oblivious. She has a small, pink plastic shopping trolley and is busy filling it with cars, books, and a teddy.

Thankfully, I'm not staying the weekend. Tula is my escape as mum doesn't like dogs in the house.

Exhausted, but full of mum's cottage pie, I wave goodbye to them all. Sighing with relief as they disappear from the rear-view mirror. I'll miss them but I know they'll have a great time and I really need a break. During the two-hour drive home alone, I replay the shocked reactions of my parents, when I told them. "Pete left weeks ago, and I don't know where he is"; and how I crumbled shamefully confessing it's not the first time and he's usually with another woman. I feel utterly pathetic for putting up with him for so long, I had willingly succumbed to mum's smothering embrace. And remembering my dad's stunned expression as he whispered, "The bastard." I dissolve into tears again knowing he never swears. Then I rant about what I'll say to Pete when I eventually get the opportunity.

Considering my emotional state, I arrive home safely and take Tula for a well- deserved walk. The next morning, I boil a ham shank, making pea and ham soup. There's also enough for sandwiches. I leave Tula with the ham bone, whilst I go for my first look at the allotment. It's freezing cold but my spirits soar when I see the plot. It's full of weeds, but a good size and there's a really nice shed with a window there.

It's raining heavily when I walk back through town to visit the new shop called 'The Pantry.' Basically, you pay a couple of quid to join, it sells short dated or damaged produce at a fraction of the price, reducing waste and landfill. It's a great idea.

Last week the mums from school had been talking about it at the gate. Today is the opening and I can see some of them inside. As I enter all chatting stops, or was that my imagination? Stella, Jessica's mum rushes over all smiles and gushes "Sally, look at this bread mix twenty-five pence. You're only allowed two, but the bakery stuff is free today, so I'll pop them away till next week." The floor is stacked with trays of assorted loaves and other baked goods. I fill my basket, along with wilted veg, and an assortment of cans with ripped or missing labels, bashed and dented, their contents are a mystery and I smile knowing the kids will love the fun of picking one and discovering what's for tea. Paying with the windfall tenner, I'm amazed the total spend is only £3:75. Staggering out with our bags we giggle.

Stella suggests we go for a coffee, then seeing my hesitation adds "it's my treat." Embarrassed I don't argue, we find a table and chat about baking. Excitedly I mention the allotment and promise her some homegrown produce.

Curiously she doesn't mention Pete, but I'm getting the impression that she and the others already know about my situation - or am I just paranoid?

The next day I'm feeling much more positive. I'd slept well, and the rain had stopped.

Me and Tula set off for our first day digging.

The Allotmentiers are a thoroughly decent bunch. Everyone chats, some bring me seeds, cuttings, even a stool and an oil lamp for my shed. I work hard all afternoon and am rewarded with a clear six-foot rectangle of soil. I'm tidying up when Stella appears.

"Hi, thought I'd find you here, it looks great." She smiles, "I've made a flask of coffee and a quiche from those short-dated eggs and stuff we got yesterday. In fact, I made three," she says smugly.

In the shed, Tula's dozing on some old potato sacks. She sits up and sniffs at the quiche as I unwrap it, so I give her a biscuit and she settles back down. I light the oil lamp, which fills the shed with a warm glow and I move the box of weed killer with its ominous skull and crossbones and perch on the window ledge.

"It's so cosy." Stella smiles, then blurts out, "I know Pete's left you and the kids." She looks uncomfortable, continuing "My friend knows who he's living with" she waits for my reaction. I don't say anything, so she goes again. "Do you want to know?"

I stare blankly not knowing the answer myself.

In the morning, I ring mum and dad and chat to the kids. All are having a great time, and the kids ask if they can stay longer to go through the illuminations. I feign reluctance. "Erm, okay but only a couple of days." They all cheer.

So, I have another couple of days and nights to sort things out. Determined to do what's right for the kids and myself. I send a simple message.

"Pete, we need to meet up."

Then I get back to work on the allotment.

The night before I collect the kids, I invite Stella for tea, to thank her. She's been so supportive, encouraging me to make appointments to discuss benefits and entitlements and has even helped me to budget. We sit around the kitchen table and tuck into a delicious sausage casserole, cauliflower cheese and a grown-up pudding, Tart Tatin. All made with the produce from The Pantry and contributions from the Allotmentiers. Stella has brought a nice bottle of wine.

"You could make meals and cakes from the stuff off your allotment and see if The Pantry would sell them," she says, spooning more rich sticky pudding into her bowl. "Make money whilst helping the planet." We both laugh, but she's right - I could. Then she changes the mood, asking solemnly.

"Did you go and see Pete?"

I shake my head. "I thought about it but I'm not ready yet. Thanks for telling me where he is, and I will go and confront him, soon." I take another sip of my wine. "Well, you may have missed your chance, my friend says he's moved on!" "What, where's he gone?!" I shriek.

"Apparently a couple of days ago he told her he was going to sort things out so they could get married. He borrowed money and her car. Guess what? He didn't come back. She found the car the next day at the train station." Pausing to take another gulp of wine she slurs.

"My friend Angie said her friend was shocked: she thought he was serious about them, but then he sent her a text saying 'Thanks for everything but I'm moving away for a new start. Sorry."

"Ha! I wouldn't put it past him to have two on the go at the same time. Well, good riddance. I hope I never see him again."

Oblivious she persists "I know I said to Angie, if he'll leave his wife and 3 kids, he'll leave her once he's spent her money, and I was right!"

Picking up the wine bottle I find it empty. "I need to make us some allotment wine." I giggle. "Let's have a coffee, you go into the lounge."

As she leaves the kitchen a little unsteadily. I turn to catch my breath stifling a sob, leaning against the worktop, shoulders hunched. I fight to regain my composure.

Then I carry in the tray heavy with homemade cookies, cheese straws, the cafetiere and a little jug of cream.

~~~

Thanks to mum and dad, Christmas is good. We have a delicious dinner, and the kids want for nothing. Only Charlie mentions his dad once, saying "I hope he's got us some nice presents when he comes back," then disappears into his room with his game station, whilst the other two play happily together.

Mum whispers, passing me another mince pie.

"You must never be short of anything darling, me and your dad will always support you. The kids are better off without him and so are you."

I nod thoughtfully.

~~~

Spring sees the allotment come to life. The kids love spending time here and each of them has their own patch. Today we're having a 4th birthday party for Grace. Stella and her children help transform the shed with balloons and bunting. My parents arrive with folding chairs.

There's music, party games, hotdogs, a homemade birthday cake and the weather's amazing.

Colin and Jean appear from the next plot. Whenever I need to borrow a tool or have a problem, they come to my rescue. They've brought Grace seeds and a cute little gardening set.

"All your hard work has paid off, your soil wasn't great, but you've got results" Colin nods at the abundance of sprouting greenery.

Feeling very proud I answer, "Yes, I added peat as you suggested." I'm horrified at my unintentional confession.

Then Jean chips in with an air of finality "Well that's the end of Peat."

I look vacant. Do they all know I've poisoned my cheating husband and buried him under the cabbages? Feeling faint I struggle to regain self-control. "What do you mean?"

"Peat. Next year it's banned. It has a negative impact on the environment, we need an alternative," she says, all serious.

I'm so relieved and stunned for a second. Then my dad starts a discussion about the degeneration of peat bogs releasing carbon dioxide and what alternatives there are. "I've read about it in the paper. An anaerobic digester is what you need, and you can use lamb's wool to hold the moisture in the soil."

I think they're a bit taken aback by my sudden high pitch laughter, and my over enthusiastic nodding. "Yes, yes, of course," I say joining in. "Lamb's wool, that'll do the trick," whilst hugging my wonderful dad. Then I offer everyone more cake and give Tula a nice bone.

In the new days

by Fiona Mischel

J odie was up first. This was unusual—normally Da was up early
to feed the fermenter. But today the kitchen was quiet and the
fermenter was blinking an unhappy red.

Jodie crossed the room, carefully avoiding the worn patch down
the centre where the microbes in the concrete were still repairing the
floor. She looked up at the fermenter on the countertop. It was still
winking down at her forlornly from its shiny steel face. She scrambled
up, her little legs struggling for a moment in empty air. Standing on
the counter, she was only a little taller than the fermenter herself. Of
course, this was just the household one. The big fermenter out by
Mum's workshop was taller than Da. She pried open the lid with a
child's deft fingers and looked inside. All the cartridges were empty.
If Da didn't come down soon, there wouldn't be enough time for
the fermenter to cycle by dinner time. No cycle, no cells. No cells, no
supper.

Carefully, Jodie closed the lid and hopped off the counter. She
opened the fridge and pulled open the family's cell bank. Little vials of
chicken cells were nestled next to cow and pig. Her favourite was the
salmon but the little space where the vial should be was empty. They
would have to get some more cells from their family's salmon, Algie.

For a moment, Jodie didn't know what to do. She could load cells into the fermenter and they could have nice beef steaks for dinner. But if she wanted to grow steaks instead of ground meat, hadn't Da said the cells needed different nutrients? Or no, maybe that was for fish. Steaks were a setting. Yes, the scaffold setting so the meat would have a 3D structure.

Jodie hurried back to the fermenter and popped the lid. She couldn't read yet, but she thought that long word might be *scaffolding*. But it could also have been *cyanobacteria* and Mum wouldn't be happy if she ran an algae cycle on animal cartridges. "Stops up the works," she had said.

At five years old, Jodie was old enough to go with Mum to take the cell samples from their animals like Algie and Little Jo, their slow-moving cow who made them milk in the mornings. But Da said she still couldn't touch the fermenter. This was frustrating because most of her friends had toy fermenters and they used them all the time. "They're too expensive," Mum had said.

But Jodie didn't complain too much because most of her friends didn't have any family animals and Mum said their family was extremely lucky. Jodie agreed, especially about Little Jo. She loved her gentle eyes and the way she smelled and the slow way she swung her head. The cow also wasn't as frantic as their chicken, Dumb-Dumb, or as insistent as Eddie, their potbellied pig and Jodie found that very comforting.

Just looking at the empty fermenter made her hungry, so she closed the lid and popped open the bottom tray. There were strips of raw bacon there, ready to be fried. Maybe she could surprise Da and cook them all by herself.

Carefully, she climbed back off the counter, grabbed a fork out of the drawer and speared the bacon from the tray into a frying pan. She flicked on the electric hob and waited for the bacon to sizzle. She was just wondering if she should turn them over when there was a clack and thud of feet on the stairs and Da came rushing into the kitchen.

"Whoa there!" he gasped. "What's going on here?" "Making breakfast," Jodie replied.

Da scooted her out of the way and turned down the heat. "Next time you want to cook, come get me first, hmm?" He ruffled her hair, gently took the fork and flipped over the bacon. They looked a bit black on the underside, Jodie noticed.

"Why were you late?" she asked, looking up at his crinkly, bearded face. His eyes were so bright and blue that Jodie always imagined they could see through everything around them.

"Nothing to worry about, little sprout. Mum and I were just talking about the soil. The microbes aren't happy again and we don't know why. Not storing as much carbon as they should."

"But isn't that the trees' job?" Jodie wondered.

"The trees can't do it all by themselves," Da said patiently. "The little organisms you can't see take on just as much of the work."

Jodie nodded even though she didn't really understand. Mum and Da were always worried about microbes. Sometimes it was the ones in the soil or the ones in the big fermenter. Sometimes it was the ones all over the counters and then Mum insisted they wipe them away.

"Why don't we make Mum some toast and cheese and bring her this bacon you've cooked up, hmm?" suggested Da.

Jodie trotted over to the bread and handed it to him for slicing. Then she pulled open the fridge and took out some of last week's fermenter cheese. Once, Mum had said they could use some of Little Jo's milk to make cheese like they did in the old days before fermenters did all the work. "But Little Jo only makes enough milk for the three of us," Mum had warned. "Cows don't have to produce as much as they did fifty years ago so we won't get much cheese."

Her parents' room was at the top of the house. The biosensor on the landing—no bigger than Da's hand—showed green. The air was good today, then. Mum was sitting in their bed that she had made herself out of fabricated wood from the big fermenter. It was a nice reddish brown and covered with big cosy blankets. Mum had grown all kinds of fibres in the big fermenter so some of the blankets were cotton, some linen, and one was even wool. Mum couldn't knit very well but at least the wool was soft.

Mum looked tired. Her dark curly hair was bound up in her sleeping scarf and there were lines on her face that Jodie thought hadn't been there before. But she smiled at the sight of her daughter in the doorway and Jodie jumped exuberantly into her arms.

"What a lovely breakfast!" she exclaimed as Da handed her the plate. "Jodie, did you make this all by yourself?" she asked, suddenly suspicious.

"Da helped," said Jodie quickly.

Da nodded helpfully and sat down on the bed as Mum tucked into the bacon. Jodie thought she might have winced at the black crust on one side but maybe she imagined it.

For a while, Jodie listened to Mum and Da talk about the soil and why its microbiome was unbalanced. Da had put sensors in the ground last week and some of the microbe strains were over-producing. It was very boring but Jodie liked being with Mum and Da in the big bed, so she didn't mind.

"I'll get the cells going for dinner and then I'll get out there," Da was saying. "You take a lie in."

"I'll be fine," Mum said impatiently.

"What's wrong?" Jodie said, looking up at her.

"Nothing, little sprout. Too much work, not enough tickles!" she said, and Jodie squealed as her mother tickled her and covered her in kisses. Then Da joined in and Jodie escaped and Da chased her around the room and then she chased him back and then they both jumped back on Mum and the last of the toast went flying.

They lay there for a moment, panting and laughing and feeling much too warm on Mum's wool blanket. "I'd best get going," said Da reluctantly.

Mum nodded and Da got changed into his work clothes. His hair was standing on end like it had been electrified and Jodie laughed at him.

"Well," said Mum when Da had gone. "Will you help me with the animals today? Da says the cow cell lines are wearing out and we need new ones."

"And Algie," she added.

"And Algie," Mum sighed. Jodie knew she didn't like taking cells from Algie. They had to do it while he was underwater, of course, which Mum said was "a giant pain in the—." But where it was a giant pain, Mum would never say.

Mum got dressed and helped Jodie into her clothes. After a small fuss in which Jodie didn't want to wear a coat and Mum made her anyway, she followed Mum out to the farm.

Their family lived on a big patch of land that Mum said had once been an industrial site. It had not been a nice place then, so they had gotten the land at a bargain. That was before all the land had been cleaned up, so Mum and Da had had to do a lot of it themselves. That's also why Jodie's parents were older than most of her friends; they'd waited to have Jodie until after the land was restored.

Jodie helped Mum take the big bucket of feed out to Little Jo, who lowed at the smell of barley and lumbered over to greet them. Jodie patted her black and white splotched face and her soft, snuffly nose.

Mum had brought along the syringe kit to take some of Little Jo's cells. "Does it hurt?" Jodie had asked once.

"Only a little pinch," Mum had said. "Like when you get a shot at the doctors."

Jodie thought that hurt quite a lot so now she always fed Little Jo extra barley when Mum took a biopsy.

"Why don't we get all our cells in the mail like Fatima's family?" Jodie asked as Mum sterilised a spot on Little Jo's haunch.

"We could," Mum said. "But I grew up by a farm and I always liked taking care of animals. We don't need to keep so many animals now so most of that land has gone back into forests. But I think it's nice to have our own little farm. Little Jo is more than just her cells," she added.

Jodie agreed and kissed Little Jo and told her that she was the best cow in the whole wide world. Little Jo replied with a slobbery lick of her rough tongue like a giant cat. After a few moments, Mum said that she was all done, and they could take the cells back to the processor. Jodie looked up, startled. Little Jo hadn't even flinched.

They took Algie's cells next. Jodie held Algie underwater in his net while Mum muttered a lot under her breath. By the time they were done, Jodie was bored and wanted to play hide-around-the-bushes.

"Not right now, love," said Mum. "I'm too tired." She did look a bit sick and her voice, always so rich and warm, sounded thin.

"Please, Mum!" Jodie whined.

"Not right now, I said," Mum replied in the tone Jodie knew not to argue with. "Go inside and I'll be in soon."

When Jodie was gone, Nadia sat down heavily, her chest heaving. She didn't want her daughter to see her like this. Not yet. But the day was coming when she wouldn't be able to hide it any longer.

She looked out across the lush green land and felt the same surge of pride she always did.

She had dedicated her life to restoring the damaged places of the world, the water that had festered with chemicals, the heavy metals that had poisoned the soil. But it had come at a cost.

Ewan said she should tell Jodie what was happening. "She'll be proud of you," he insisted.

"She'll be scared," Nadia replied. "She shouldn't have to know these things."

"One day, she'll know everything. She'll learn about it in school, what the world was, how close to the brink we came. She should know what her mum did. What she sacrificed."

"It wasn't a sacrifice because it wasn't a choice," said Nadia hotly. "It's where I was born."

Ewan wrapped her in his arms and kissed her brow, saying without speaking that he was sorry, sorry for what she had lived through and sorry for how he had misspoken. That he loved her more than all the stars in the night. That he was scared, too.

"I know it wasn't," he said softly.

Her generation would be the last, the exposed children whose lungs and blood, whose very DNA had been broken in their earliest years. There was a small comfort in that, mixed in with all her anger. But more than anything, Nadia wished she could watch her daughter grow up.

Her breath was back and steady in her chest and, after a moment, she followed her daughter back into their house.

The rest of Jodie's day was a good day except for the part where she fell and skinned her knee and the other part where she wanted to play in the mud with Eddie the pig and Mum wouldn't let her.

Da was home late that night which was just as well because the cells in the kitchen fermenter didn't finish cultivating until well after sunset. Mum fed Jodie an extra snack but she was still tired and generally unhappy by the time dinner was served. Tonight was pork sausages. There hadn't been time to run the scaffold setting which meant no pork chops. But Jodie didn't mind now that her belly was full.

Then it was time for bed which Jodie suddenly decided she didn't want to do. Da played with her while Mum put her feet up and read the news. But after what seemed like only five minutes, Da insisted it was bedtime. Jodie didn't want playtime to end and started crying, which, in Jodie's mind, was a perfectly reasonable thing to do. Then Da got upset and Mum told him to take a break and promised she would tell Jodie a story if she brushed her teeth right away and got into bed. Jodie loved Mum's stories more than anything, so she scampered off to find her toothbrush. Da's hair was standing on end again.

Jodie's room was her special place. It was full of little glowing plants that Da had gotten from the baby store in town. Jodie wasn't a baby anymore, but she treasured her plants even if she couldn't pronounce *bioluminescence* very well.

She heard Mum coming up the stairs and jumped into bed. Mum smiled when she opened the door. She was carrying a warm cup of milk from Little Jo and Jodie scooted over so Mum could cuddle her while she told her a story.

"Do you want a new story or an old story?" Mum asked. Jodie sipped her milk and thought about it. The milk was rich and creamy and reminded her of Little Jo's big nose.

"Tell me the first story," Jodie said after a moment. "About before I was born."

Mum smiled and rolled her neck. Then she began in that soft voice Jodie loved so much. "Before you were born, the world was a very scary place. Human beings hadn't been kind to the Earth and the Earth was angry. There were terrible storms and heatwaves, and many people and animals were hurt."

"But you fixed it," Jodie interrupted. She didn't like this part of the story very much. "Yes," Mum said gently, "We fixed it. Millions and millions of people all over the world wanted to save the Earth and everyone that lived on it." "People like you and Da?"

"Like me and Da, exactly. Many, many people built solar panels and wind farms and other people took the dinosaur fossils out of cars and planes. Some people built the cell fermenters like we have in our kitchen and made them small enough so everyone could have one."

"And some people made the bad land better!"

"That's how your Da and I met," Ma said, her voice even softer now. "We were taking samples of the land all around this house and we saw that it was very sick. But we also knew that if we added tiny, special microbes into the dirt they would eat up all the pollutants and make the land healthy again. And so that's what we did. It took a long time but when we were done, we built our house."

"And then you had me," Jodie interrupted again even though her eyes were closed. "And then we had you," Mum said and kissed her curls and tucked her into sleep.

Break Glass

by Sarah Woods

It catches her every time, the wind. She stands bracing herself against the central staircase, taking a few minutes to look out towards the horizon and allow herself to hope. She fancies she can see something, a shape in the sky, movement in the water. Of course, this is wishful thinking. There is still work to do.

Below the helipad, where they have extended the array of solar panels, she doesn't need to go far to see that the seawater has not receded. It laps over the rig floor, everything down below is unreachable, unless you fancy a swim. The marks for the high tide point show it hasn't come any higher, so there is that. She makes a mental note.

This is her fourth rotation, and she has learned that there is no point in trying to write down anything until she is safely back inside. Will she ever get used to this cold? Still, for all the buffeting and the rain that lashes horizontally, getting into her eyes, this is her one chance of fresh air a day.

She takes in lungful after lungful, tasting that ozone, remembering walking along St Andrew's Quay, with Dad, off to B&Q, past the monument to the trawler men lost at sea. Those two-dimensional statues, frozen in time; men, their trawler and the seagulls that follow in its wake, ever hopeful for their share of the catch. They're all underwater now too, the sea defences breached, as anyone with half a brain could've predicted. *Wait*.

Against the howling of the wind, she tries to focus her hearing. Was that a screech, the once familiar cry? She peers up at the Meccano-like structure of the derrick. But there's nothing there.

Teeth chattering, Alessia tugs open the heavy metal door and throws herself, wind-assisted, inside. There's a loud clang that echoes through the empty space. She peels off the layers of rubber boots and orange hi-vis revealing the hood of her dry-suit. It pokes out above Dad's old, Shetland sweater which is like a dress on her. She shucks it over her head and struggles out of the cumbersome dry suit. Sweat has dampened her double layer of clothes, she knows she will soon feel the chill, and slips the sweater back over her clothes. Nothing is easy on the rig.

Outside checks done, she heads for the control room. Her footsteps echo with a metallic ring, you can never forget where you are. The space is sparsely furnished but there are plenty of past riggers' ghosts to keep her company. They've left messages in the abandoned books, electric shavers and photos of loved ones.

She's found a diary.

It's a short walk to the nerve centre of operations with its comforting hum of technology, monitoring everything and maintaining the systems. A ghost rig where everything was abandoned when the waters rose. She checks the readouts and it's all stable, thank goodness. Time for a brew.

On her way out she stops beside the secured metal box. It's what she was working on, in the before times. She knew her employers didn't care if it worked; it was a token gesture, a sop to the environmentalists. But to her…? To her it's personal. She unlocks it and looks at the array of sealed metal canisters, chunky and solid, with their lids screwed on.

There's another seal inside. Someone, with a sense of humour, had written on them: *In Case of Emergency Break Glass.* She reaches out and touches one as if for luck and says a silent prayer.

The kettle clicks. Thank goodness for the solar panels she smiles to herself. Greenwashing, from years back, replacing the generator with the latest iteration; so effective that, even in these low light level days, it's enough. More than enough for one person.

Time to phone in.

He picks up the call immediately. She looks at herself on the tiny screen and runs her fingers through her unkempt hair.

"Alessia, you okay?"

"I'm good Pete, don't worry about me." She smiles, holding the phone up to a more flattering angle. "Nothing to report. How are things there?"

"Good news!" His face cracks into the broadest, white-toothed grin, "The fish are coming back."

"Fantastic! So soon?"

"Yes, the bio-plankton reactor is working better than we dared to hope. We're pumping out algae and the zooplankton is back to normal levels. It's still early days and everything is so fragile in this environment but, you're not going to believe this, cod have been spotted near the rig!"

"In the North Sea? No way!" It is better than they had ever hoped.

"Yes, I know! Nature just needed us working with it and *voila*!" He holds his hands up like a magician's assistant.

"That's the best news," says Alessia. Their eyes are shining in the illumination from their screens. She wishes she could reach through and touch him. His warm, honeyed skin, her fingers in his soft curly hair.

"And there's more good news." He pauses for dramatic effect, ensuring he has her full attention before announcing, "Tomorrow, I'm coming out to join you!"

Her eyes are saucers, "But, how?"

"Jim's re-rigged the Serendipity. I'm sailing out first thing. I hope you haven't broken all the glasses. I'm bringing a bot_"

The screen goes blank. She wills him back but the signal is lost. Transmitter interference, meteor shower or loss of power on his end, she doesn't know. *He's coming tomorrow.*

Alessia pulls the neck of her Dad's old sweater away from her body and sniffs. Okay, time to up the desalination plant output and set the water heater for a shower in the morning. It wouldn't normally bother her, going a fortnight without a wash, but this is a special occasion.

Tucked up in her cabin bed, she can hear the wind howl and the drumbeat of the driving rain. There are no windows out here, she has gotten used to that. The tiny light fixed to her headboard is enough to read the pages of the diary. It doesn't begin, *this book belongs to John aged fifty-six and three-quarters,* so she doesn't know whose words she is reading. She assumes it is a man; the technical details, the unwavering decisiveness, the lack of emotion, that is, until the final entry.

She likes to think it's her dad's. It isn't, but it was somebody's dad for sure. The day-to-day tedium of life on the rig, the twelve-hour shifts, she didn't know, he'd never said. In fact, they hadn't talked much about his job. She regrets that now.

Tomorrow, she will do her checks and imagine the fish that are not far from where she stands, perhaps even swimming beneath her right now. A silver hoard, a treasure whose price goes far beyond soft, shiny metal. A shoal of cod. Her mouth waters, remembering Friday night treats; the salty vinegary taste, a parcel to unwrap, trays balanced on knees in front of the telly. It was a different world.

The rig reacts to the rise and fall of the sea, like a ship. She has grown so used to it she barely notices. Built to withstand whatever the elements can throw at it, she feels safe, cocooned, lulled even. Alessia turns off her light. In the total darkness, she watches the different shades of grey-tinged orange behind her eyelids. One more sleep and he will be here. She will not have to dream of him, but for now, she cuddles under the duvet and relaxes.

The claxon beats her over the head, dragging her from sleep. Her eyes squint at the flashing orange light. "Jesus," she mutters, pulling herself out of the warm, safe nest. She stumbles into her thermal onesie, jeans and pullover, telling herself it's a false alarm, an electric circuit tripped, a power out.

In the corridor, the lights are always on day or night. The persistent siren pierces the usual calm. She makes her way to the control room and throws the switch. Silence. Yet, the warning lights are still flashing.

"Okay, okay, what's wrong?" She talks to herself, a bad habit that's getting worse.

Her finger runs across the screens checking the information, seeing where the fault is. Oh, God.

There's a breach.

Initiating emergency protocol, she sets in motion the underwater cameras to locate the problem. With the joystick between her fingers, she runs the camera up the shaft of the dormant drill pipe. A cloud, like smoke, swirls across her view. The picture darkens, but not before she has seen the jagged edges of the burst pipe. There is no time to think, *will it work?* She has to act.

The door flies out of her hand. Bright white LEDs illuminate the rig and bounce off the ink-black water. She's wearing her diving mask, already steaming up. The smell, like burnt creosote, fills the air. Even in all her layers, the cold is biting, her hands numb inside the protective gloves gripping tightly to the canister.

She moves towards the edge of the platform, wading knee-deep in water. She rams into the edging rails. Pinned as she is, the sea grabs hold of her, pushing then pulling at her shins and calves, probing for a grip to drag her down.

She focuses her head torch onto the viscous plume of darker darkness. Her heart rate doubles and moving her head, as if she were relieving a pain in her neck, she traces the spreading circumference of the blackening circle. The light bounces off its surface, an iridescence that in other circumstances would be beautiful. It's expanding so rapidly. There is no time.

"Okay, you've got this."

In the canister, the various different microbes, only ever used in the controlled environment of the laboratory, are held in stasis. They have been engineered and modified to be the most efficient they can be. Designed for this very purpose, but never even trialled in the field. Once the waters rose and the drilling was forced to stop, there seemed little point. Still, each rig had its own secured canisters, a safeguard no one believed would ever be used.

She thinks of the fish. Against all the odds, they fight back to survive, to regain their place in a damaged food chain that the team, her team, are trying to repair. Link by precarious link, restoring the thoughtless damage. Now she must do her part. It is time to break the glass.

The wind picks up its pace snarling around her, whistling through the derrick. The night is black. No stars peep through the blanket of swirling cloud. Thoughts of her dad are in her head. *"If the helicopter ditches, let's practise. Big breaths, Alessia. And again, and again."*

She felt light-headed. There was a strange tingling in her body, and lights flashed in the corners of her vision. *"Now, hold your breath!"*

Her small hands clamped over her nose and mouth, copying him.

His eyes bulged, looking up, left and right, as if it were all a joke. Blood pumped through her neck and thrummed loudly in her ears. With rising panic, she couldn't do it any longer. She gasped, deflating, falling forward but he carried on. And on. And on. His face was red, perspiration across his cheeks and nose. The numbers on the timer he had set whizzed higher and higher.

"Daddy, stop it! Stop it!" She hit him with her tiny fists punching his arms until he stopped, grabbed hold of her, and took a gulp of air.

"Look, a minute and seven seconds. Not bad for an old bloke. The thing to do, chicken, is not panic."

He lifted her up in his strong arms and rubbed his bristly cheek against her soft face.

Tucking the canister under her arm, she climbs over the railing. One leg carefully after the other. She feels the coldness as the sea rises up her legs, over the dry-suit. She should've put on more layers. The canister is held tightly to her chest. With her free hand she attaches her tether and takes deep breaths, filling her lungs with the foul smell, and then she jumps.

She floats, of course she does. Around her, the oily waters cling to her dry suit and splash her face mask. The icy cold forces all the air from her lungs. Deep breaths, deep breaths. Alessia closes her mouth and pushes herself under the water.

Her headlight barely pierces the gloom. She's lucky, the tide is with her. She lets it drive her forward, not sure of her speed, until she clatters into the drill pipe forcing precious air from her lungs and the canister from her hand.

In a blind panic, she fumbles for it but everything is slower in the water. Her fingers frantically reach out, grab - she has it!

But she doesn't know where she is, she can't see a thing. Her empty lungs beg her to return to the surface. *Don't panic.* She closes her eyes and feels the crude oil pummelling her cheeks.

Alessia grips the pipe with her legs, anchoring herself. She reaches up and feels for it. It's there, right in front of her, the jagged edge of the gaping hole. She unscrews the lid imagining the grating sound she cannot hear. Inside the contents are protected by a fragile, glass seal. Here with the pressure of the sea, she feels it has broken and thrusts the canister into the hole.

"Ahoy!"

He stands on the deck of the Serendipity, waving both arms above his head. Alessia, warm in her layers, her skin scrubbed raw in the shower with Swarfega, she feels the sun on the top of her head. She stands ready to catch the rope, to haul him close enough to disembark.

Below the rig, she sees the water swell, rising and falling. There is the slightest aroma of menthol in the air, but that is dissipating too. Her aching muscles are readying for action, the sun doing its trick to keep her awake.

"Look what I've got," he shouts, holding up a bottle, its cork covered by a wire basket and foil cap. When did she last taste Prosecco, let alone champagne? Then, from just above her comes a once familiar cry.

Perched on the spindles of the derrick, buffeted by the wind, she isn't imagining it, it's really there. "Look!" she shouts and points.

Pete puts a hand on his forehead to shade his eyes and turns to where she has directed his gaze. The beady-eyed seagull isn't looking back, - no, he's too busy. With his keen vision, he's spotted them. He's watching the silvery shoal as it swims through the crystal clear waters of the North Sea. Then he opens his wings and follows.

The Pitch

by D.A. Baden

*T**his is a stand-alone extract from the novel 'Habitat Man' that reimagines the start of the story.*

I rehearsed my pitch on the train all the way to Waterloo, drawing strange looks from the couple sitting opposite, who were no doubt wondering why my mouth was moving silently and my eyebrows were wavering between imploring, glowering and deadly serious.

At Waterloo, I approached the usual mix of homeless, beggars and Big Issue sellers, rummaging in my pocket for change. The smart-suited man ahead of me made the mistake of giving a fiver to the bolshy guy at the end. I'd noticed the more money he was given, the longer his tirade would be.

'Fiver wouldn't even pay your dry-cleaning bill, you rich tosser,' Bolshy Guy hurled at him, deftly pocketing the note.

Smart-suited man shook his head, shuffling from polished black shoe to polished black shoe as the tirade continued.

'The world would be better off if you didn't exist. If you didn't bother with your dry-cleaned suit and stayed at home and did sweet fuck all. Smart-guy-city-tosspot,' he accused, peering up through overgrown eyebrows and shaggy hair.

He had a point. I'd calculated the environmental impacts of laundry using the Costing for Nature software and could have informed them about the high carbon footprint of washing clothes and the contribution of dry cleaners to air pollution. I decided not to interject and walked on past 'smart-guy-city-tosspot', who stood patiently accepting the abuse. The tirade might go on for a while and I couldn't afford to be late. Anyway, I didn't need my daily dose of psychic self-flagellation, because today I'd be part of the solution, not part of the problem.

I walked the familiar route over Waterloo Bridge and gulped in a lungful of the bracing wind, taking in the open vista of the Thames and the Houses of Parliament etched against the cornflower blue sky. A cormorant perched on an old barge, drying its wings. Gulls circled raucously above; crabs picked among the debris on the muddy banks where the tide had receded. Nature in the heart of the city.

Last week, Extinction Rebellion protestors had occupied the bridge. Part of me had been thrilled to see them. Hordes of young, bearded, pierced, and tattooed protestors beating drums, chanting and waving banners: 'Save the Earth', 'Rebel for Life', 'Wise up. Rise up'. There had been families too, mothers with pushchairs, dads with toddlers on their shoulders. But no amount of smiles and thumbs up on my part could disguise my city suit and complicity. They'd chanted, 'this is the sixth mass extinction,' and in my paranoia and guilt, I'd been sure it was aimed at me.

I got to work with twenty minutes to spare and headed straight for the bathroom, suddenly nervous. I hated our office toilets, the scent of the air freshener worse than what it disguised. And they were pretentious, with toilets that automatically flushed the moment you got off them, or, unnervingly, when you moved on the seat. I washed my hands quickly. It must be nearly time for my pitch. I hoped Simon, the financial director, wouldn't be there with his intimidating beard. I regarded my pale, freckled face in the mirror and longed to be more hirsute. I didn't even want a beard necessarily, just the feeling that beneath my skin were follicles of thick, dark, bristly hair bursting to come forth. Then I'd feel equal to the task.

I regretted again scheduling my meeting with the carbon offsetting enterprise on the same day. If the pitch failed it would be a waste of time, but they'd been insistent.

I headed to the conference room and sat amidst the pot plants in the waiting area.

'By valuing the ecosystem and everything that depends upon it, we will protect it,' I whispered earnestly to the Areca Fern and Rubber Plant. 'Unless we cost for nature...'

I stopped quickly as several suited men and a woman trailed out, leaving Martin and Simon at the table. Through the glass walls, I saw Simon open up his laptop and show something to Martin. They talked animatedly, probably working out how inputting the environmental and social impacts of each project would affect the overall costs. Martin beckoned me in. I entered with the gait of a confident man who was bringing them the best thing since sliced bread.

'Hi there. Right, er...'

'That's us on the beach,' Simon was saying.

'Looks lovely,' murmured Martin.

'Four-star resort, but we wouldn't go back.'

I sat at the table opposite them and placed my laptop on the top pointedly. Martin eventually looked over.

'What are we meeting about again, Tim? Remind me.'

'This is to talk about the Costing for Nature software that will transform the way we do business. For the better,' I added quickly.

'Okay, go ahead.'

'We need to cost for nature.' Simon was still swiping through his photos. I paused, but he showed no sign of looking up. 'For example, when we cost a project for time and money, we factor in the carbon cost too, and allow money to offset.'

Martin looked doubtful.

'It's not a perfect solution, but at least the environmental costs would form part of the cost-benefit analysis.'

No reaction.

'My degree was in biology. I don't know if you knew that? So I've been able to feed the latest environmental data and predicted carbon costs into the algorithms.'

'Sounds expensive.' Simon finally looked up.

'No, we developed some software that calculates it for us.' I searched in vain for a sign they'd checked it out. 'There was a link in my email?'

I waited while they murmured among themselves. It was a brief conversation.

'Thanks for your idea, but it's not something we'll be taking forward right now,' said Martin.

'But—'

'We're a business, not a nature reserve.'

'But we're part of nature. Don't you see?' I searched their faces desperately for a hint of understanding. 'We're costing for ourselves!'

Martin nodded towards the door. Simon was back on his photos.

I returned to my desk, sat in my ergonomically designed chair among a sea of similar chairs and desks in the open-plan office, and gazed at my screen. The screensaver showed endless forests against a startling blue sky. I tapped a key and up came accounts for a global IT company we were helping to make richer. Standard financial modelling indicated that designing products to fail with parts that couldn't be replaced was the most profitable business model. I gazed blankly at the numbers as it sank in. They hadn't even looked at my CFN analysis that costed in the e-waste, unnecessary carbon emissions, and health costs from sweatshop conditions and toxic ingredients that seeped into the water. A new screensaver sprang up. A tropical island with clear, turquoise sea filled with colourful fish. I was suddenly furious. They hadn't looked at any of the sample scenarios. I grabbed my laptop and marched back in.

They were still there exchanging holiday horror stories.

'Bali was crap too. You couldn't swim in the sea,' Martin informed Simon.

'It's not more expensive,' I declared loudly, striding in and banging the door behind me. Well, I tried to, but it was a glass door on a hinge designed to shut gently. They watched as the door closed slowly. I picked up the clicker and moved to the next slide.

'See that,' I pointed at a graph showing two lines comparing current costs with costs using the CFN.

'What's CFN?' Simon deigned to glance over.

'It's Costing for Nature accounting software,' I told him through gritted teeth.

'Well it costs more, doesn't it?'

'Now look.' I typed three years into the time box. The two lines for standard cost and CFN costs came together. 'Now see.' I typed five years into the box and the CFN line shifted below the standard cost line. 'CFN saves money. This scenario is for the construction companies we deal with that we walk past every day coming into work. Simply switching to green cement, for example, substantially lowers CFN costs due to its lower carbon footprint.'

'I drive,' Simon said.

'What? Why would you drive?'

'I've got a Ferrari.'

I looked at him in his perfectly cut suit, shoes too shiny for public transport and hated him.

'Way overpriced for what you get. Now if it were a Porsche—' began Martin.

'But the point is,' I shouted over him, 'for every company we deal with, in the short term, yes it costs money to cost in environmental impacts, but in the medium to long term it costs way more not to.'

'I'll tell you what costs too much money,' Martin said.

'What?' Simon asked.

'A Ferrari,' said Martin.

'No, two-week holidays swimming in plastic,' Simon retorted.

'Ouch.'

I lost it. 'I don't care about your car or your two weeks' holiday on your tropical island.'

'The holiday was shit anyway,' consoled Simon. 'We had to return early. My son got asthma and the hospitals were full.'

'Don't you see we're the engines of all this?' I cried. 'Plastic didn't get in the sea by magic. The asthma didn't just happen. It was the pollution from clearing rainforests. The whole of bloody Indonesia has breathing difficulties. We crunch the numbers and depending on what goes in, out come the decisions. If we added waste and air quality and climate change to our numbers, you wouldn't get plastic in the sea and asthma. You must see that? It's us, it's all us! It's all our fault.'

They looked at me aghast as my voice hit soprano pitch. 'I'm not jealous of your Ferrari or your holiday, or your beard.' Simon looked up sharply and stroked his beard possessively. He shot Martin a look. Was it guilt? I pressed the point home.

'Surely you must see it's our fault? But that's okay, because the Costing for Nature software can put it right. We're part of nature, we're costing for ourselves. Don't you see? We crunch the numbers. What goes in is what comes out.' I knew I was repeating myself, but was unable to stop. 'We're not just complicit, we're guilty, but we can make it right!'

'Mmmhmm,' soothed Martin. I petered out, finally deciphering their expression. It wasn't guilt. It was pity.

I fell silent and packed up my laptop and left the room.

I returned to my desk and fell into my chair. Twenty-five years. I'd been in this job for twenty-five years. My fingers hovered over the keyboard, but nothing happened. I couldn't type a word. I tried to close the file I'd been working on but fell at the first hurdle. 'Save', 'Don't Save'. I gazed at the simple question. Eventually I realised I didn't care. I pushed the power button hard until it gave up the red light and set off early for my next meeting.

I walked back across Waterloo Bridge to Waterloo station where I handed the bolshy guy a twenty-pound note and passed the time by gazing at my black polished shoes as he told me at great length how the world would be better off without me.

* * *

As the business and shopping centres of Woking came into view, I realised that the pitch hadn't stood a chance. Of course they'd said no. They only cared about profits and to expect anything more was foolish. With a longer time frame, the Costing for Nature policy would save money, but who thought beyond the next quarter? On the walk from the station, I berated myself for being an idiot and getting people's hopes up. Specifically, Ian and Cathy, a married couple I was on the way to see, who were looking forward to seeing how the Costing for Nature software could link up with their carbon offsetting app.

Ian, a tall blonde man in his thirties, answered the door beaming. 'Tim! Thanks for meeting us in our home. It makes it easier with the kids.'

'I'm sorry,' I said straightaway. 'There was probably no point my coming. They didn't bite.'

Two girls rushed up to the door. 'What didn't bite? Do you mean the crickets?' the eldest asked eagerly.

'They do bite so,' claimed the younger one.

'This is Lucy and Anna. Girls, say hi to Tim.'

'Do you have crickets?' I asked, distracted for a moment from my woes.

'Loads!'

'Your garden must have excellent biodiversity.'

Ian looked proud. 'Come and see.' He ushered me inside and we followed the girls into a kitchen that led out through a patio door into a garden.

I opened my mouth to continue my apology but was immediately hushed by Lucy.

'Listen!'

We heard the unmistakable chirp of crickets.

'Do they bite?' Anna asked me.

'We just heard them for the first time today so they're all excited,' said Ian. We let our grass grow to attract more wildlife, and it looks like we've succeeded.'

'Well?' demanded Anna.

I thought back thirty years to my biology practical and the wildlife habitat we'd created in the University gardens. 'There is one species that bites, the wart-biter bush cricket. But they're very rare.'

'Told you,' declared Lucy, satisfied.

'Anyway, I'm really sorry—' I began.

'So you know about wildlife gardening do you?' Ian interrupted.

'I used to be a guerrilla gardener before I joined the rat race.'

'What did you do?'

I smiled, remembering. 'Gardens on bus shelter roofs was our thing,'

'Cool! Why did you stop?'

'PansyGate!'

'What?'

'We got overrun by the Bassett Ladies. They'd see a space that had a lovely bit of scrub, dandelions, great plants for wildlife that thrive in such conditions. And they'd pull it up to plant something pretty.'

'They sound pure evil!' He grinned and nodded over the fence. 'Just like my neighbour. If she comes out, pretend to be a wildlife garden consultant!'

I glanced over at the neat garden next door. 'I don't understand?'

'It starts with an enquiry if our lawnmower is broken and would we like to borrow theirs, but what she really means is cut your damn lawn.'

'Er...'

'If we can say we paid someone to check our garden as a professional habitat man, then that's different,' said Ian.

'Your garden already seems to be a perfect habitat for wildlife,' I said, looking round. The grass was quite long. Garden debris piled up by the side, providing a habitat for invertebrates. Half-buried logs for the vertebrates, water butt, a swift box under the eaves.

'Look.' Lucy led me towards a small pond shining in the corner.

'We want frogs but there aren't none,' said Anna.

'Any,' corrected Ian, 'there aren't any.'

'That's what I said. There's no frogs.' Anna looked at me as if I could fix it.

'Their numbers have fallen, due to habitat loss and water contamination mainly, but also predation,' I said.

The girls looked bemused. I rephrased. 'They need a good place to live, and your pond is great, except for that open patch between the pond and the hedge.'

'Is that bad?' Lucy asked.

'Some birds eat frogs so they'd be exposed here. They like to travel without being seen so no one can spot them and eat them.'

The girls looked suspiciously up at the sky.

'Let the grass grow extra long between the pond and the hedges to provide cover for them.'

'Good idea.' Ian nodded next door where the neighbour had appeared to hang out her washing and spoke loudly. 'We should keep our grass long you say?'

I raised my voice slightly. 'One of the easiest things a gardener can do to enhance the wildlife value of their garden is to mow the lawn less frequently.'

'We're hoping to grow a meadow.'

'For a meadow, you'll only need to cut the grass and compost the clippings once a year, in late August.'

'Thank you for your professional opinion as Habitat Man. We'll do as you say.' He winked at me.

'If you allow your grass to grow, daisies, clover, buttercups, and dandelions will naturally proliferate, creating a meadow-like effect. For a wider variety like poppies, cornflowers, etc. remove some turf round the edges and replace with some horticultural grit or sand mix and sow wildflowers there,' I proclaimed, getting into my role as Habitat Man. 'Yellow rattle will reduce the vigour of the grass, giving other wildflowers more of a chance. It wouldn't be long before your garden is alive with all kinds of butterflies.'

'You're good at this. I'm impressed.' Ian pointed towards an intriguing wooden hut perched on a raised patio area at the bottom of the garden. 'This will impress you.'

'It's a cool design. Is it a shed?'

'Come and see.'

Anna and Lucy followed us. 'Do you want a wee?' Anna asked.

'Or poo,' giggled Lucy.

Ian laughed. 'This is our composting toilet.'

It was beautifully designed. Almost an arch shape, with a circular stained glass window towards the top of the door to allow in light. The way it curved into a point gave it an ethereal Lord of the Rings look.

'I've heard of these, but I've not been in one.'

He looked at me expectantly, so I opened the door and beheld the toilet. It was small but stylish – a square box painted in red, gold and white.

Ian's face burst with pride. He lifted up the slab of wood that the toilet seat was set into. Underneath were two compartments. At the front was a large plastic bottle and at the back, in a separate section, was a square plastic container lined with a large bag and half full of wood shavings.

'We have a twin-bowl design that separates the solid from the urine, to keep it dry so you don't get flies. It goes dry and crumbly when it meets the oxygen and the aerobic bacteria breaks it down into germ-free compost, so you only need to empty it about once or twice a year, and you can use it to revitalise the soil.'

'This is Ian's new toy.' A friendly-looking woman joined us. 'You must be Tim. I'm Cathy.' She held out her hand.

I took it and remembered why I was there and my failure. My stuttered explanations were interrupted by Ian, who was desperate for me to try his toilet.

'When you go, you use toilet paper as usual, then instead of flushing, you put down two scoops of wood shavings. No water, no chemicals. It doesn't smell at all, does it?'

'No it doesn't.'

'Would you like a go?' He nodded, bright-eyed.

'Maybe later.'

'I'll just top up the wood shavings, in case.'

Cathy laughed and rolled her eyes. 'We'll leave him to it. Tim, come have a coffee.'

Once inside, the mood lift I'd experienced in the garden disappeared, and I was left again with a feeling of despair. While Cathy made coffee, I filled her in on how the pitch had gone.

'I didn't think they'd go for it. There's nothing compelling them is there?' Cathy put a cup of coffee in front of me.

I gulped it and burnt my mouth. I spat it back quickly and panted open-mouthed like a stranded fish.

She poured me a glass of cold water. 'It's not your fault,' she said, watching me gulp it down. 'Businesses seek profit. Unless we change their legal form and make them all social enterprises or benefit corporations, they'll do what's best for their shareholders.'

'But shareholders are people too! They want clean water, fresh air, a future for their children.' I had an image of business as a moth blindly rushing towards the bright, hot lights of profit, taking humanity with it to its doom. I barely looked up as Ian joined us with the girls, realising the implications with a sudden gut-churning certainty. 'We don't stand a chance.'

Cathy frowned, and Ian spoke up briskly. 'Girls you go play outside, we're working in here now.'

'I didn't mean to scare them.'

'It's okay.' Ian sat at the table with us. 'In our day we worried about nuclear war. Kids today worry about climate change.'

'But this is inevitable. It's chemistry. Ice melts at zero degrees. It's not a might happen or it might not,' I cried.

'This generation isn't so ingrained in the old ways. We hope they'll help tip us over into the right mindset,' said Ian.

'One day they'll be in power, then things will change,' Cathy said.

'But it will be too late.' I could barely get the words out. Tomorrow I would be fifty. I'd spent half my life in that job. It was just the hope that my company would go for the Costing for Nature software that had kept me going. Could I put my shoulder back to that grinding wheel of commerce? Mid-life crisis, right on time.

'Our carbon offsets are making a difference. These projects are literally drawing down carbon and pulling it out of the air.' Cathy's tone was desperately reassuring.

'But they're voluntary – it's a fraction of what's needed.'

'We're putting everything in place,' Ian assured me.

'Before we can regulate, we need to be able to calculate the carbon footprint of everything,' said Cathy. 'Carbon offsets normalise the idea that businesses and governments can offset to get to zero. Consumers can use them too, so they don't feel guilty.'

'But you're right,' Ian admitted. 'Until it's mandatory and everyone has their own carbon allowance, it won't touch the sides.'

'How do you go on?' I was desperate for an answer.

'Hope. There comes a point when it's obvious to the majority that we have more to lose than gain by business as usual, and then the changes will come fast. Look at the NHS and welfare state. Concern about poverty and ill health built over centuries, but when we made the move, we did it within a decade.'

'The Australians chose the greenest politicians after all their fires,' Ian added.

'Look at the Cuban revolution. Look at glasnost and perestroika, when the Soviet Union changed almost overnight. As long as the pieces are in place, change can come rapidly once the tipping point is reached, when we all realise there is more to lose than gain,' Cathy said.

'It's like gardening. Prepare the ground, before you plant the seeds,' said Ian. 'I think of our wildlife garden as an island of plenty, a haven so that when we come to our senses and nurture nature, then there's some left to start afresh.'

I nodded to be polite, but he was kidding himself. This was just one garden. Our most likely future presented itself to me with a sickening clarity. They must have thought me so naïve. My guts were twisting as I struggled with the indigestible truth. I could hear the girls giggling as they crept into the kitchen, and it broke my heart. How we fool ourselves, believing what we want to believe.

'If you knew my pitch wouldn't work, why did you agree to see me?' I asked suddenly.

'We seed ideas as well – not just about offsetting, but like the composting toilet,' said Ian. 'Soon we won't be able to waste precious fresh water. Flushing away our waste, creating sewage that mixes with pesticide and agricultural run-offs to contaminate our rivers – it's unnecessary. So I show everyone my wonderful composting toilet – seeding the idea because the first step is to raise awareness, make people more familiar with them and how they work.'

'Basically, Ian wanted to show you his new toilet,' said Cathy.

'Are you sure you don't want to go?' He looked at me hopefully.

I didn't trust myself to speak and just nodded.

Ian smiled delighted. The girls jumped up to follow me, but he held them back.

'Leave him in peace. It's his first time.'

'Have a nice wee, Habitat Man,' shouted Anna after me.

'Or poo!' Lucy added.

I left the sounds of laughing children and escaped outside. But there was no escape from the turmoil in my head. Thoughts bashed against each other in my besieged psyche like bumper cars at the fair. How can I go on? What else would I do? Lose myself in drink? Retreat into denial? Was that even possible?

The freshness of the air gradually calmed my ruminations. A few slow soft drops of rain started then petered out. The sun emerged, setting the raindrops sparkling against the vegetation. I peeked over the fence at next door's neat garden. Ecologists would call it a green desert – a tightly mown lawn, bedding plants round the border, non-native shrubs. Bamboo, Japanese maple and rhododendron may cut a dash but have nothing to offer local wildlife. The grass would have been heavily treated with weed killer to look so pristine, perhaps explaining the lack of insect life.

The quantities of toxins we were pouring into our soil, rivers and ponds alarmed me. It wasn't just agriculture that was the culprit, but shop-bought pesticides, slug pellets, weed killers, even pet treatments. The Costing for Nature software would have revealed their true cost. Soil that was once biologically active, teeming with life and the building blocks of our whole ecology was turning to lifeless dirt, increasingly incapable of sustaining the thriving ecology we needed for our food and health.

A sense of futility hit me again like a punch in the stomach and I returned to the glorious abundance of shelter and food in Ian's garden. The comparison was stark, and I saw now what he'd meant by an island of plenty. I heard the sweet melody of a song thrush – increasingly rare these days. There it was on a branch near the pond, waiting for me to leave so he could pop down to the pond for a quick wash and dinner of midges. The brief spell of rain had released the smell of the lavender from the borders, attracting the bees. A tortoiseshell butterfly fluttered around the buddleia.

I entered the composting toilet and sat down. The feeling of calm and sanctuary inside echoed the garden. It was perfectly quiet except for the distant sound of a wood pigeon. It smelled of forests and fresh air, soothing to the senses and the spirit.

The notion of islands of plenty stirred a faint memory of my ecology module many years ago. Something to do with pockets of resilience – the idea that you can create refuges, or was it refugii? Maybe Ian was right. If you can create enough safe habitats, then wildlife could repopulate an area once conditions improved. If just a fifth of UK gardens were kept pesticide-free, and grown with native plants suited to local invertebrates, you'd have an area the size of Luxembourg. It just might be enough.

I'd want to chop down non-native species like bamboo and replace with a native deciduous tree, maybe a hawthorn with berries for the birds and nesting sites. A pond for sure. Pollinator-friendly plants for the bees and butterflies. Everyone's into the idea of keeping honey-bees, but they were out-competing wild bees, so I'd create habitats for mason bees. They'd be happy with a few bamboo canes tied together, and they'd hide out in the holes. Ladybirds would be content with pinecones shoved together in with some dried leaves. No need to buy compost – each garden would make their own, with food leftovers, mixed in with garden debris and their own waste.

The smell of wood shavings reminded me of the hamster I used to keep. Trapped in its cage, running endlessly on the wheel. I thought of my job and the office toilets. But here there were no harsh lights, whirr of fans, smell of urine overlaid with air freshener. Instead, daylight streamed in through the small window, which I now saw had a picture set into the glass, a frog on a lily pad amidst dragonflies and bulrushes.

The sun caught the stained-glass window and brought the scene suddenly to life, creating an almost religious experience. The elusive frog so sensitive to water pollution, safe here where our waste was used to nurture life. I heard the chirp of a cricket and smiled. In the sanctuary of the composting toilet, at last I forgave myself. One person couldn't change the world, nor should they be able to. I'd done my best within my zone of influence. It hadn't worked, but perhaps I'd planted a seed – prepared the ground as Ian would say. Maybe when conditions were right, they'd change their mind. As for what I did now?

Habitat Man. That was what Ian had called me.

I realised with surprise the decision had been made.

I breathed out for what seemed like the first time in years and relaxed. I felt a swelling up, a feeling of rightness, of great joy, a letting go.

I used the paper, then put two scoops of wood shavings down the toilet and used the hand sanitizer. I opened the door and walked out into the garden and back into the house.

Ian recognised something in my shining face and nodded, satisfied.

The Polyamorist

by D. A. Baden

*T*his is an adapted chapter from the novel 'Habitat Man' about a
man who gives up his city job to become a green garden consultant.

I heaved my way up the hill on my bike, turned into Dawn's road
and leant the bike against her fence. With the sound of my bike si-
lenced, there was a slight hush in the air. The birds seemed to sing extra
loud, calling their mates back to the nest. I allowed myself a moment
to savour the peace, marvelling at how a few trees and the sound of
birdsong and wind rustling through branches can transform an urban
suburb into an oasis of calm.

A comfortably plump, black-haired woman answered the door,
wearing multicoloured silk pyjama bottoms and a loose shirt that
exposed a generous cleavage.

'Dawn?'

'Habitat Man?' She looked me up and down, her eyes glinting, then
she beckoned me in.

I smiled nervously and followed her into the house. I'd always associated Highfield with academic types, and the very proper ladies from
the Highfield Women's Institute. They certainly wouldn't answer the
door wearing pyjamas.

'What would you like me to do?' I asked, once the kettle was on.

'I'm looking for a compassionate way to get rid of rodents.'

'Ah. I try to preserve wildlife and habitats. I'm more about how to get animals into your garden.'

'Even rats?'

'No. Rats are social and intelligent creatures, but they can easily take over.'

'I thought I had mice, so I tried to trap them with this.' She showed me a small plastic bottle with a tiny toy plastic ladder stuck to the side and a lump of cheese in the bottom. 'But it turned out to be rats.'

I jumped when she pulled a huge dead rat out of a bag by its tail.

'I called the rat man, but he just took the mick and wanted to poison them.'

I stifled a smile. The rat was many times larger than the bottle.

She dropped the rat back in the bag and handed me a mug of hot tea. I took it gratefully, glad of a chance to gather my thoughts after the misunderstanding.

'Erm... what would you like to see in your garden?'

'Hedgehogs perhaps? I haven't seen them for ages.'

'Wonderful, we can try.' I stood up, tea in hand. 'Shall we have a look?'

Dawn swapped her fluffy slippers for wellingtons and led me outside.

'First thing is to avoid slug pellets and pesticides, they're a key cause of decline of many species, hedgehogs included.' I followed Dawn into her back garden.

'Also, they need to gain access.' I looked around. The fence on one side had come down, presumably blown over by the recent storm.

'Would you consider a hedge here? It won't provide an instant barrier, but it has several advantages.'

'Do tell.'

'Firstly, new fences are often coated with a wood preserver which hedgehogs often lick and will poison them. You can get environmentally safe water-based products, but even if you do, hedgehogs need to roam, so if your garden is fully enclosed like this one, there's no space for them to get in, or out. Three, hedges are good for providing habitats and food for birds and bees.'

'Birds and bees, yes...' Dawn's eyes gleamed as she held my gaze.

'Last thing is to create a nesting site, a compost heap would do the trick, and would also provide a habitat for the kinds of creatures hedgehogs like to eat.'

Dawn shook her head. 'Apparently, it's the compost bin that's attracting the rats. I'd better stop putting in food waste.'

'Don't do that. Everything biological should be composted.' I saw her compost bin hidden in the corner of the garden. 'Let me take a look, I can probably rat-proof it.'

'I like a man that's good with his hands!' The glint in her eye was suddenly pronounced.

I was saved from having to respond by the doorbell.

She rushed inside. 'Back in a mo, hun, you do your thing.'

I checked out the compost bin. The ground underneath was uneven, allowing rats access.

When she returned, I told her my plan. 'Move the bin onto the paved area in front of your shed, then the rats can't get in. It also makes it easier to shovel out the compost from the bottom.'

'It could go there, no problem.'

'Then use the area where it was to pile up your old leaves and garden debris to create a safe spot for hedgehogs to nest.'

I lifted the lid of the compost bin. It was almost full. 'It would only take half an hour to empty out the compost, re-site the bin, and re-add the compost.'

She glanced up at the bedroom window. I wondered who'd been at the door.

'That would be wonderful.' She handed me a spade, propped up against shed.

Oh. I hadn't meant to imply I was going to do it myself. I looked at Dawn's silk pyjamas and sighed. 'Okay. I'll give you a shout when I'm done?'

I was conscious of her eyes on me as I dug out the compost and put it in a pile. I hoped I didn't have builder's bum. I straightened up and lifted my arms in the air to stretch out. Dawn's eye strayed to a patch of hairy stomach that had appeared as my shirt lifted in the stretch. I felt myself blushing and bent over the bin again. I prayed fervently she didn't plan to stand there watching me work.

'Okay, cheers, hun. I'll be upstairs. Shout when you're done.'

Thankfully, she headed inside. Lugging the top level of food scraps and grass cuttings over to the paving slabs took a while. I took the opportunity to shovel out the rich fertile compost from the bottom of the bin and pile it up round the back of her hedges, plants and trees. Once it was empty, I dragged it over to the paved area and shovelled the top bits back in. Taking out the compost and putting it back would do it good, creating pockets of oxygen that would help the process along. I noticed some lovely reddish-brown, wriggly worms left on the ground and popped them in. Job done!

I peered in the compost bin satisfied, and amazed, as always, by the chemistry that translates grass cuttings and food waste into rich, earthy soil that nourishes the garden. And it was all down to microorganisms. If I were ever to write a poem, it would be to them or the humble earthworms. Their intestines providing an incubator for microbes, working with them to digest the plant matter, then casting them back in a soil food web. Their tunnels of air, castings and water, weaving a life-giving magic. Its slimy undulations turning the waste of the world and plain mud into rich, textured soil, food from which the roses can grow. The humble worm! I replaced the lid and raised my arms above my head to stretch, then brought them slowly down, breathing in the invigorating autumn air. I dreamt of a world where we award this humble worm all the respect it deserves. I had a brief mental image of the worm with a medal round its neck, nodding modestly to the applause.

Pleased with this vision and my work, I trudged up the garden feeling the pain in my back from the bending and shovelling. I rotated my hips clockwise and then anticlockwise to ease out the kinks. I gazed up to stretch my neck and noticed a net curtain twitch in the bedroom. Was I imagining that eyes were upon me?

I opened the back door. 'Hello!' I ventured. No answer. I took off my boots and stepped into the kitchen. I was desperate to wash my hands, but the sink was full of washing up.

I heard a television on upstairs. Who else lived here? Did Dawn have a husband or family? After so many years dealing with numbers, I was finding it strange being in other people's homes.

I walked up to the bottom of the stairs. 'Hello! Er, Dawn!'

An upstairs door opened, and I heard the television more clearly. Dawn's face appeared.

'Hi, Dawn, I'm done, can I clean up?'

'Of course, hun, up here, the bathroom's on the left.'

I hastened into the bathroom to wash my hands. I emerged and jumped in shock as a piercing scream came from the bedroom. Dawn was standing in the doorway, unperturbed.

'Kerry and I like to snuggle up in bed and watch an Agatha Christie.'

I nodded, heart still racing from the unexpected scream. I could hear Miss Marple in the background. 'You are in dire peril, my dear.' Dawn was still standing there, gazing at me steadily with that glint in her eye.

'Has the Wizard been in touch?'

'Who?'

'From Woolston.'

'I've had a Geoff from Woolston.'

'That's him. Tell him I said "blessed be".'

Oh my days! He wanted bats and frogs. What was he planning on doing with them? I remembered that one of the collective nouns for bats was a cauldron of bats. Her next question brought my wild imaginings to a sudden halt.

'Fancy coming in to play?'

Play? Monopoly? Scrabble?

'Me and Kerry have been watching you and we think you're sexy.'

So I hadn't imagined the glint. The question crossed my mind whether Kerry was a male or female. Best not to ask in case she took it as interest.

I looked at my watch. Why did I do that? Now she's going to think it depends on how much time I have. Frantic sounds from the television ended my paralysis. 'You had better get away from here as fast as you can!' urged Miss Marple. I took her advice and ran.

Afterword

We'd love feedback on how you enjoyed the stories if they impacted you in anyway. The questions will help us to decide which stories to keep in future editions. Data may be used as part of an article on the impacts of eco-fiction. Scan above for survey, or visit https://southampton.qualtrics.com/jfe/form/SV_3wmKAaDQWVTzOYK.

 Sign up to the mailing list on www.greenstories.org.uk to keep informed about new writing competitions, green stories publications and research findings related to storytelling for the planet. Also connect on: facebook.com or instagram at greenstoriessoton and @GreenStoriesUK. If you enjoyed this book, please help to spread the word by leaving a review on sites such as Amazon and Good Reads. For more information about the editor go to www.dabaden.com or connect @DABadenauthor.

ACKNOWLEDGEMENTS

Thanks are due to The Environmental Biotechnology Network who sponsored the short story competition and to the authors who applied their imaginations and came up with such a diverse and intriguing selection of stories.

About the authors

Brian Adams is a Professor Emeritus of Environmental Science and the author of three romantic comedies (*Love in the Time of Climate Change, KABOOM!, and Offline*). Adams lives in Northampton, Massachusetts in a net zero energy house with his wife and Willoughby the cat.

Helen Anderson is from Australia and has always been fascinated by words, word puzzles and scrabble games. After winning a local short story competition, she fell headlong into her writing journey.

Denise Baden is professor of sustainability at the University of Southampton UK, and writer. Previous publications include: *Habitat Man, No More Fairy Tales: Stories to Save Our Planet*, and her play, *Murder in the Citizens' Jury*. She founded the Green Stories Project and is on the Forbes List of Climate Leaders Changing the Film and TV industry. https://www.dabaden.com/

Laura Baggaley is a writer of young adult fiction. Her debut novel, *Enough*, will be published by Neem Tree Press & Unbound in 2025 and is available for preorder.

Alexandra Burkitt is a postgraduate researcher at the University of York, working on the ecology of microbes in peat bogs. She combines a love of the natural world with an enthusiasm for writing, and is interested in the ways we tell stories about the nature hidden all around us.

Jenni Clarke is a multi-genre writer, and mixed media artist, born in the UK, living in France. She has won three short story competitions and has two in anthologies. Visit her website to find her published books and artwork

Adrian Ellis is a London-based writer of science-fiction, fantasy fiction, and non-fiction. His latest books are the fantasy comedy "Faery Hero No" and "How Humanity Must Survive".

Rab Ferguson is the author of the award-winning Middle Grade series "The Late Crew", about young carers meeting aliens. He also works at the amazing National Literacy Trust!

Alyson Hilbourne has been writing short stories in her spare time for many years. She has been published in magazines, online and in several anthologies. She has had several pocket novels published by DC Thomson which are now with Ulverscroft as large print reads.

Catherine Kerr is currently a student studying in the UK. She writes short stories and songs when she's supposed to be sleeping. Her current life goals include living in a castle and surviving med school, the latter of which seems more impossible. She thanks you for taking the time to read her story.

Fiona Mischel is a science communicator and fiction writer living in the UK. She focuses her day-to-day work on biotech for climate and her creative time on sci-fi and fantasy and serving the growing demands of a six kilo cat.

Jamie Mollart's first novel, The Zoo, was published in 2015 and he was made an Amazon Rising Star. His second novel, Kings of a Dead World was published in 2021 was longlisted for the BSFA awards and had a limited Waterstones edition. He is working on his third.

Dolly Joy O. Ogatis is a 20-year-old Filipina writer from the province of Sultan Kudarat, Philippines. She is a microbiologist-in-training. When she has time, she writes stories only she can read. You won't find her on social media, but you can find her in the library.

Sharon Godiff Pulido from Manchester England. Enjoys writing short stories due to being a lazy reader. Many have been included in anthologies. She has recently had a stage play produced and performed. She enjoys working in education as a creative writing facilitator. She's currently working on her first novel.

Eleanor Rycroft is a hobbyist writer living in the UK. She has written a handful of short stories and has long nurtured an interest in nature, science, and the environment.

Beatrice Smyth is an engineer who likes a good story. Originally from Donegal, she lives in Belfast where she teaches and researches sustainable energy.

Hannah Southcott is an author and journalist living on the east coast of Australia. She writes a variety of poetry, fiction, memoir, short stories and children's books.

EJ Taylor is a writer from South Yorkshire, England. Her short stories have won several competitions, and she is currently working on her first novel. Find out more at:

Prashant Vaze is an India based British writer and policy wonk. He worked as an economist in the UK civil service and publishes on energy and environmental issues. Works include The Economical Environmentalist, Repowering Communities and The Rising Tide. prashantvaze.com

Sarah Woods lives in North Yorkshire, UK with her husband and their rescue dog. She writes for adults and children and is particularly interested in the environment and inclusivity.

Printed in Great Britain
by Amazon